Jim Henson's™ FRAGGLE ROCK™

MOKEY LOSES HER MUSE

Published by
ARCHAIA™

Series Designer **MICHELLE ANKLEY**
Collection Designer **JILLIAN CRAB**
Assistant Editor **GAVIN GRONENTHAL**
Editor **CAMERON CHITTOCK**

JIM HENSON'S FRAGGLE ROCK: MOKEY LOSES HER MUSE, November 2018. Published by Archaia, a division of Boom Entertainment, Inc. © 2018 The Jim Henson Company. JIM HENSON's mark & logo, FRAGGLE ROCK, mark & logo, and all related characters and elements are trademarks of The Jim Henson Company. Originally published in single magazine form as JIM HENSON'S FRAGGLE ROCK No. 1. ™ & © 2018 The Jim Henson Company. All Rights Reserved. Archaia™ and the Archaia logo are trademarks of Boom Entertainment, Inc., registered in various countries and categories. All characters, events, and institutions depicted herein are fictional. Any similarity between any of the names, characters, persons, events, and/or institutions in this publication to actual names, characters, and persons, whether living or dead, events, and/or institutions is unintended and purely coincidental.

BOOM! Studios, 5670 Wilshire Boulevard, Suite 400, Los Angeles, CA 90036-5679. Printed in China. First Printing.

ISBN: 978-1-68415-262-9, eISBN: 978-1-64144-124-7

Jim Henson's™

FRAGGLE ROCK™

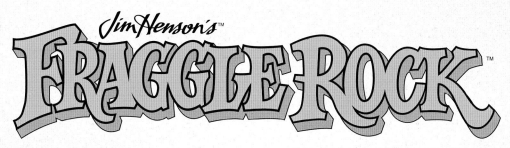

MOKEY LOSES HER MUSE

Story and Art by

JARED CULLUM

Letters by

MIKE FIORENTINO

Cover Art by

JARED CULLUM

Special Thanks to

BRIAN HENSON, LISA HENSON, JIM FORMANEK, NICOLE GOLDMAN, MARYANNE PITTMAN, CARLA DELLAVEDOVA, JUSTIN HILDEN, KAREN FALK, BLANCA LISTA, and the entire Jim Henson Company team.

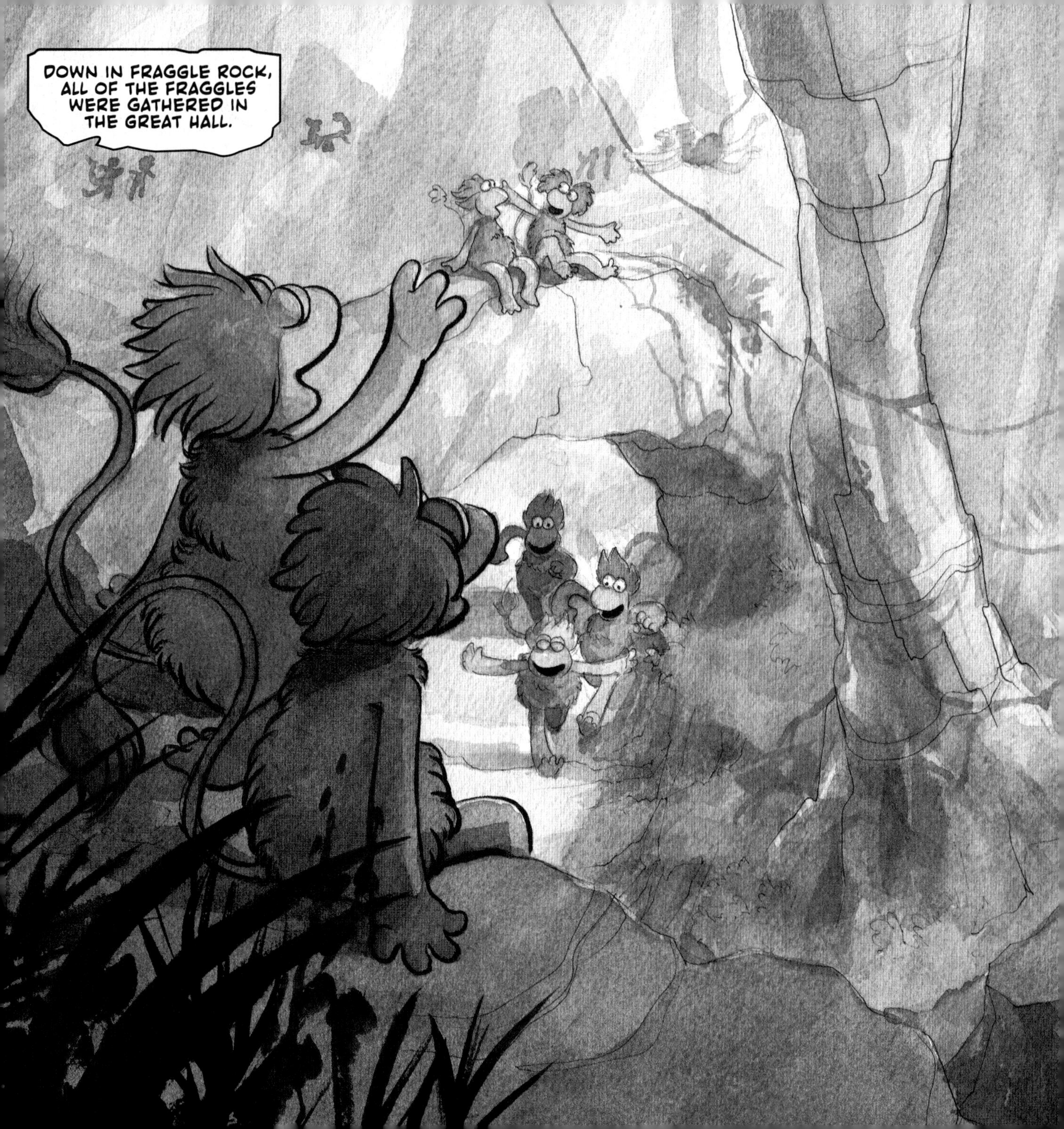
DOWN IN FRAGGLE ROCK, ALL OF THE FRAGGLES WERE GATHERED IN THE GREAT HALL.

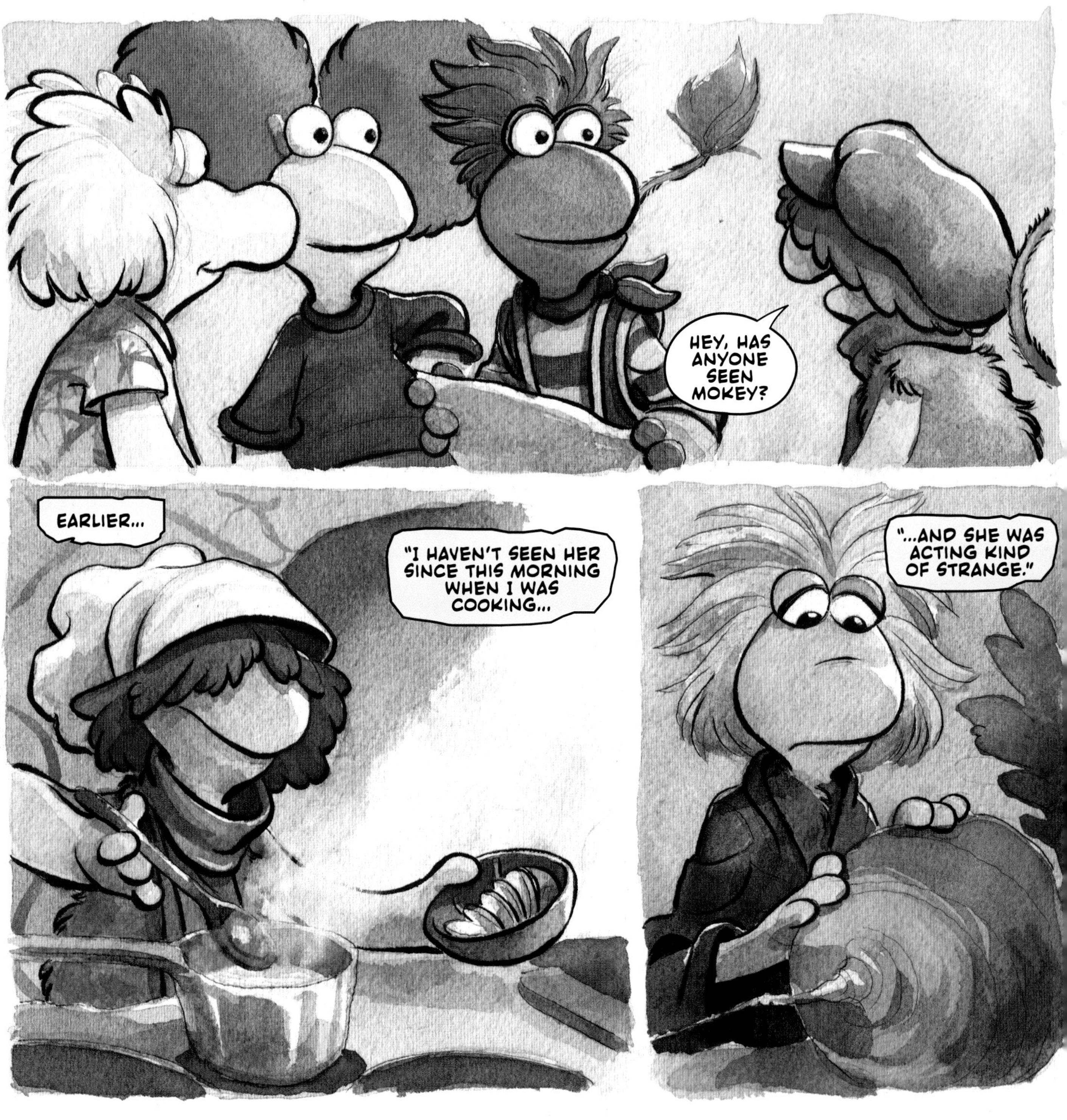
HEY, HAS ANYONE SEEN MOKEY?
EARLIER...
"I HAVEN'T SEEN HER SINCE THIS MORNING WHEN I WAS COOKING...
"...AND SHE WAS ACTING KIND OF STRANGE."

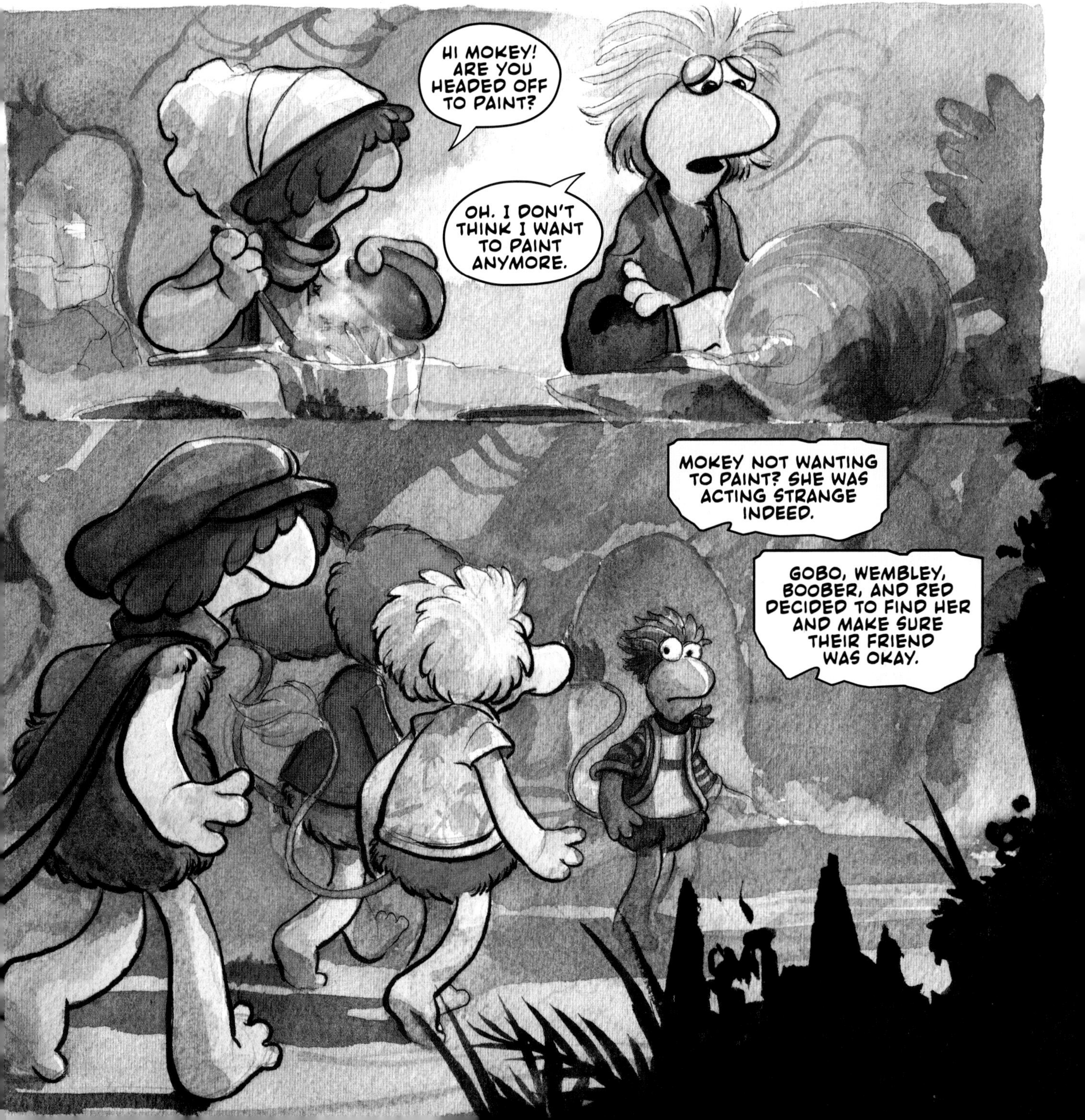
HI MOKEY! ARE YOU HEADED OFF TO PAINT?
OH. I DON'T THINK I WANT TO PAINT ANYMORE.
MOKEY NOT WANTING TO PAINT? SHE WAS ACTING STRANGE INDEED.
GOBO, WEMBLEY, BOOBER, AND RED DECIDED TO FIND HER AND MAKE SURE THEIR FRIEND WAS OKAY.

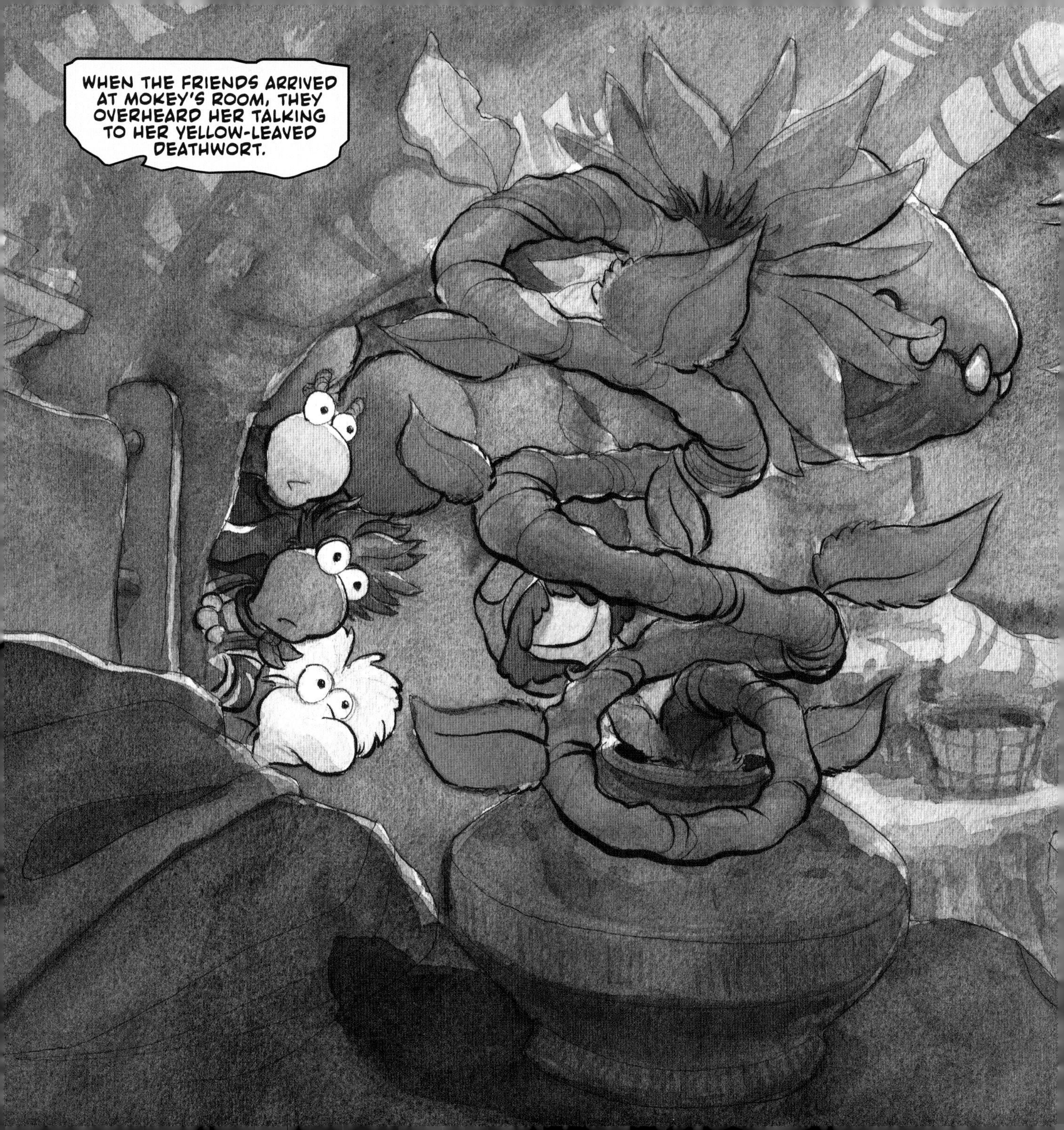
WHEN THE FRIENDS ARRIVED AT MOKEY'S ROOM, THEY OVERHEARD HER TALKING TO HER YELLOW-LEAVED DEATHWORT.

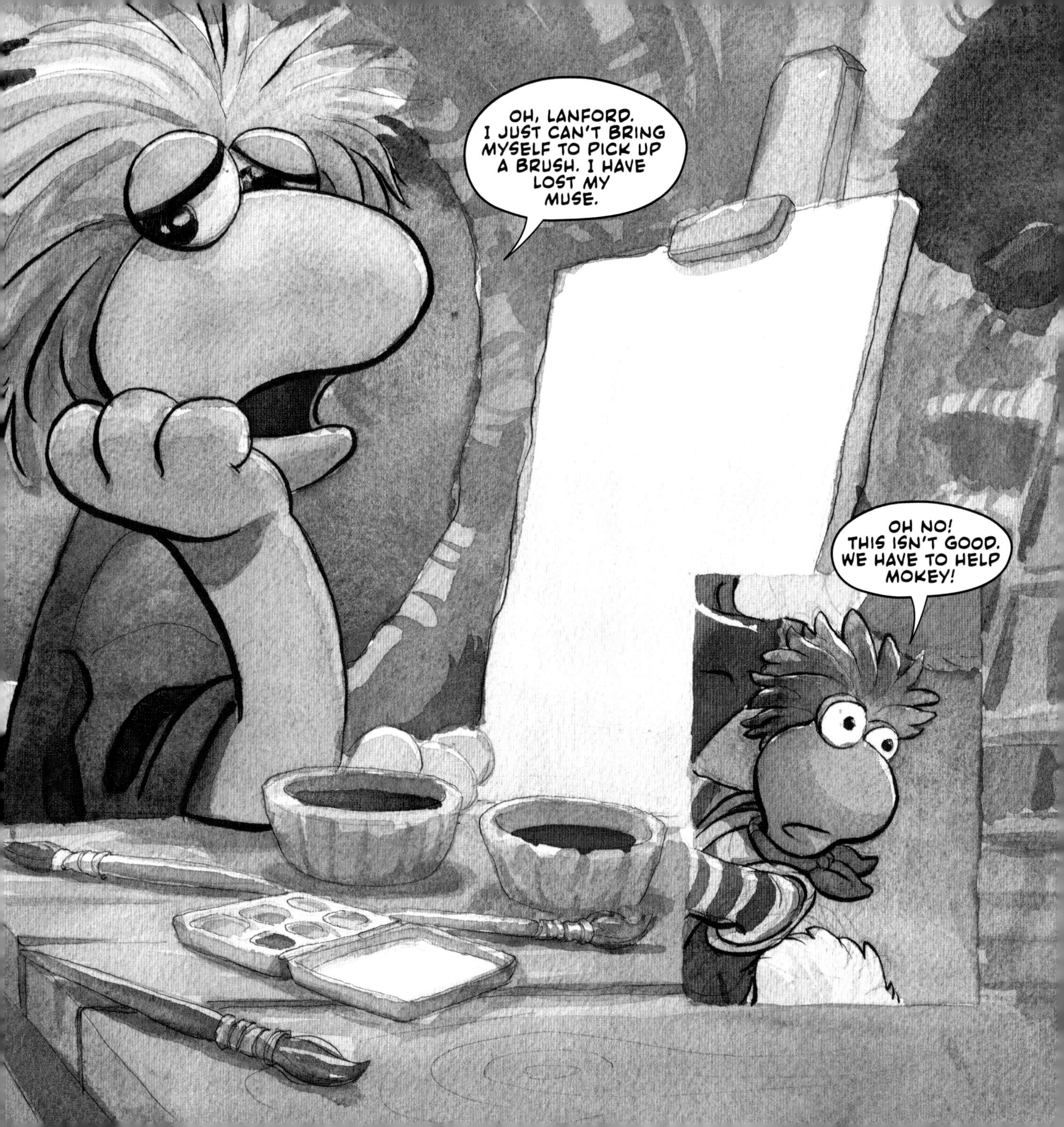

OH, LANFORD. I JUST CAN'T BRING MYSELF TO PICK UP A BRUSH. I HAVE LOST MY MUSE.
OH NO! THIS ISN'T GOOD. WE HAVE TO HELP MOKEY!

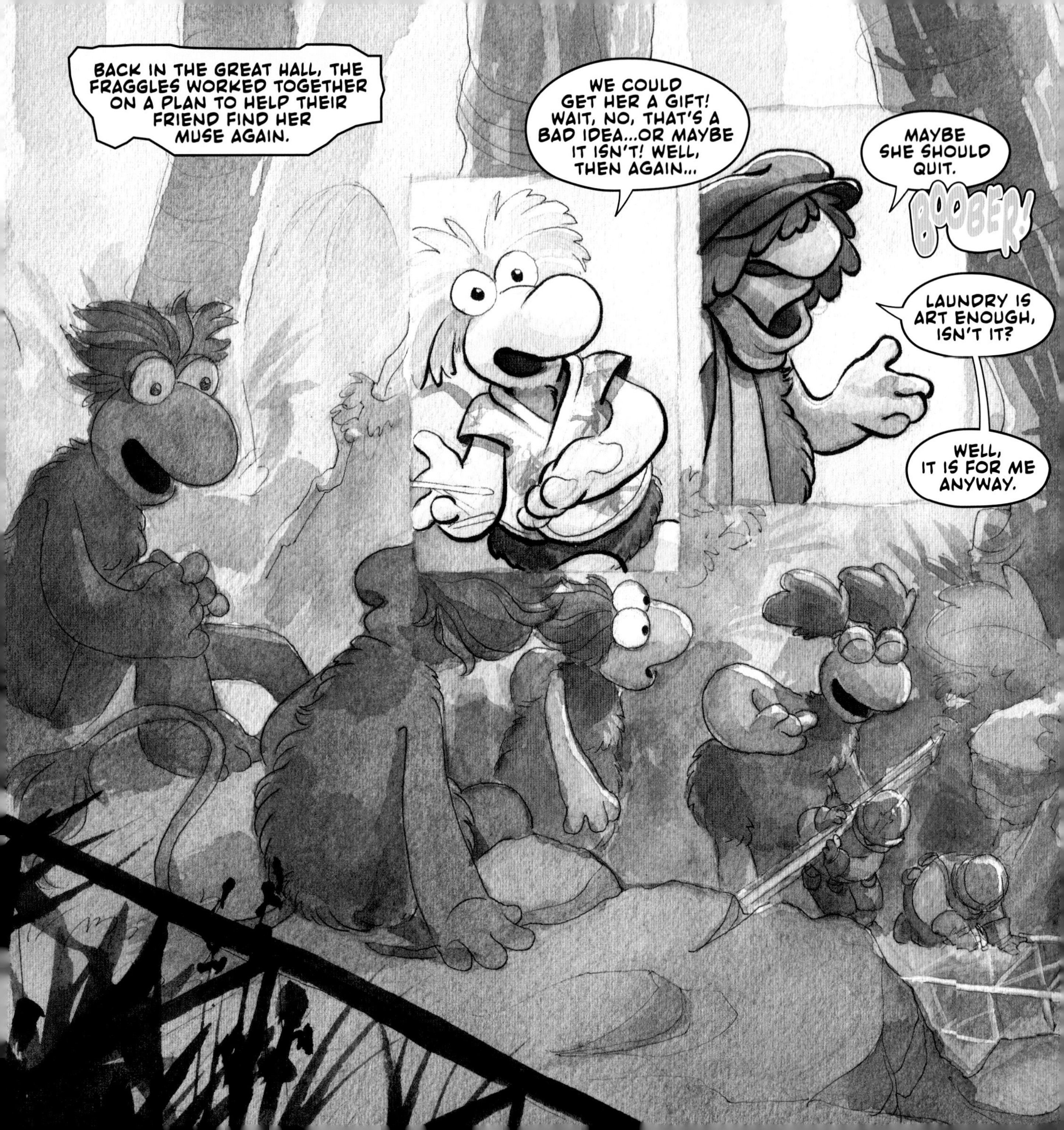
BACK IN THE GREAT HALL, THE FRAGGLES WORKED TOGETHER ON A PLAN TO HELP THEIR FRIEND FIND HER MUSE AGAIN.
WE COULD GET HER A GIFT! WAIT, NO, THAT'S A BAD IDEA...OR MAYBE IT ISN'T! WELL, THEN AGAIN...
MAYBE SHE SHOULD QUIT.
BOOBER!
LAUNDRY IS ART ENOUGH, ISN'T IT?
WELL, IT IS FOR ME ANYWAY.

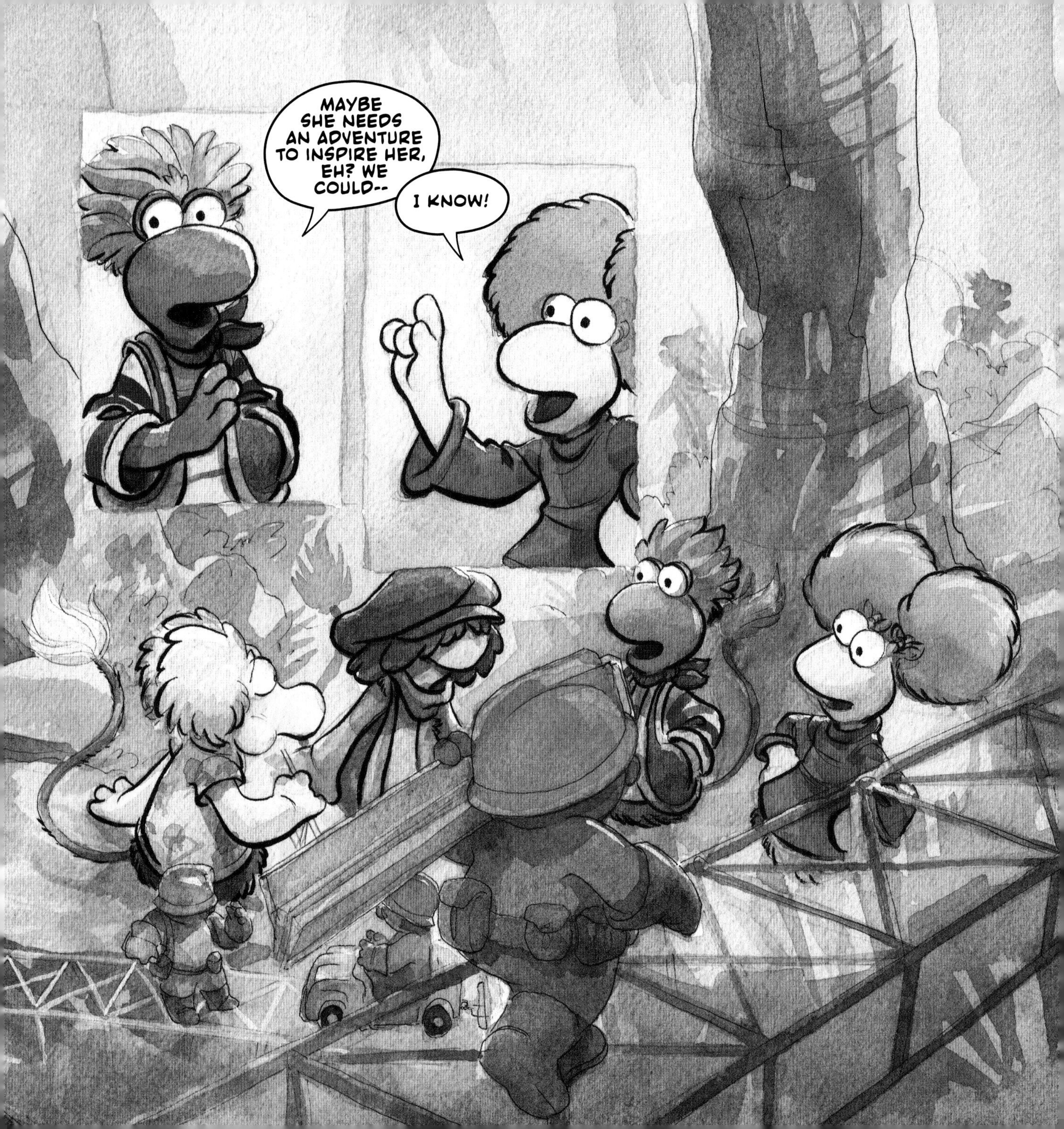
MAYBE SHE NEEDS AN ADVENTURE TO INSPIRE HER, EH? WE COULD--
I KNOW!

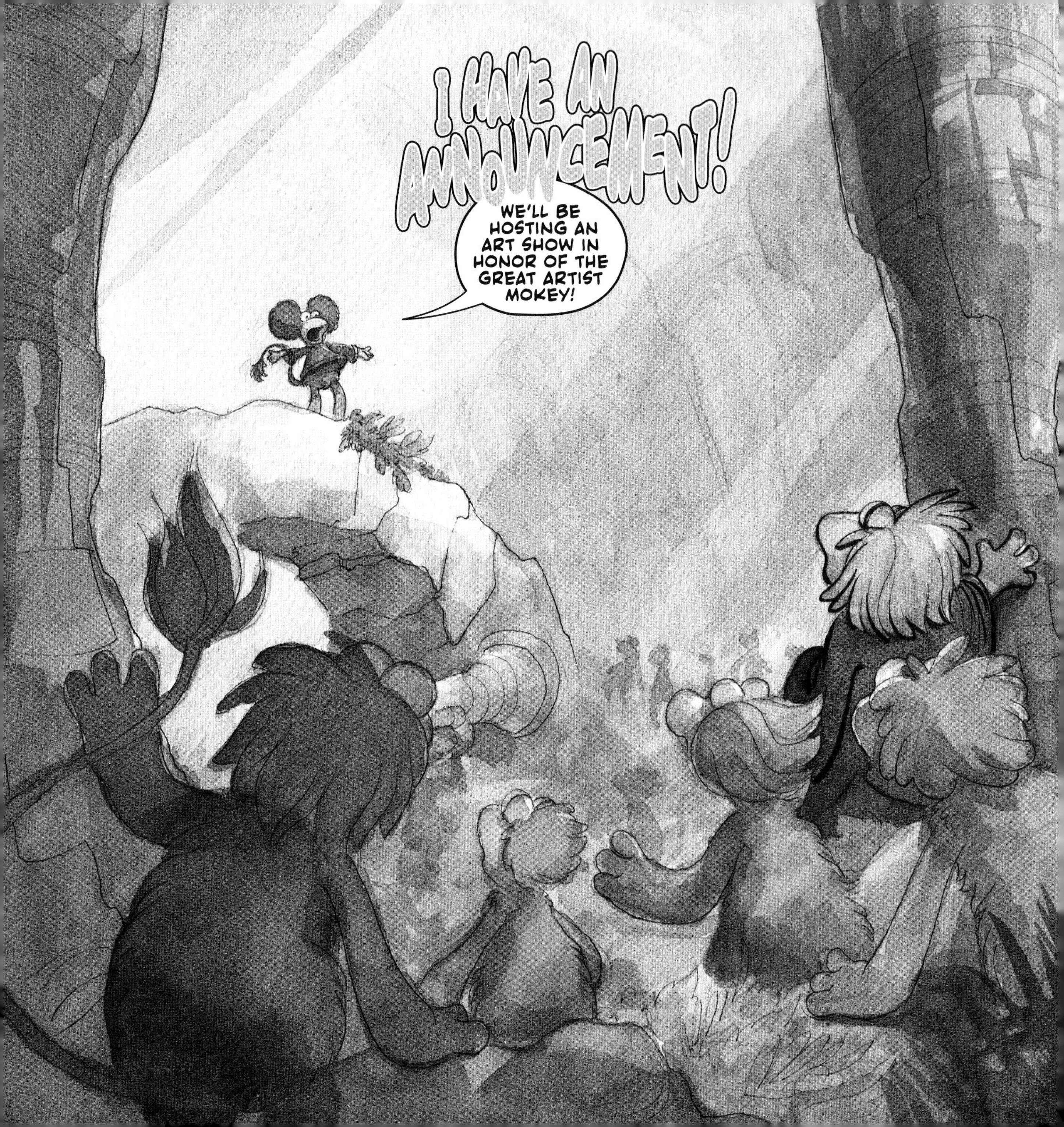
I HAVE AN ANNOUNCEMENT!
WE'LL BE HOSTING AN ART SHOW IN HONOR OF THE GREAT ARTIST MOKEY!

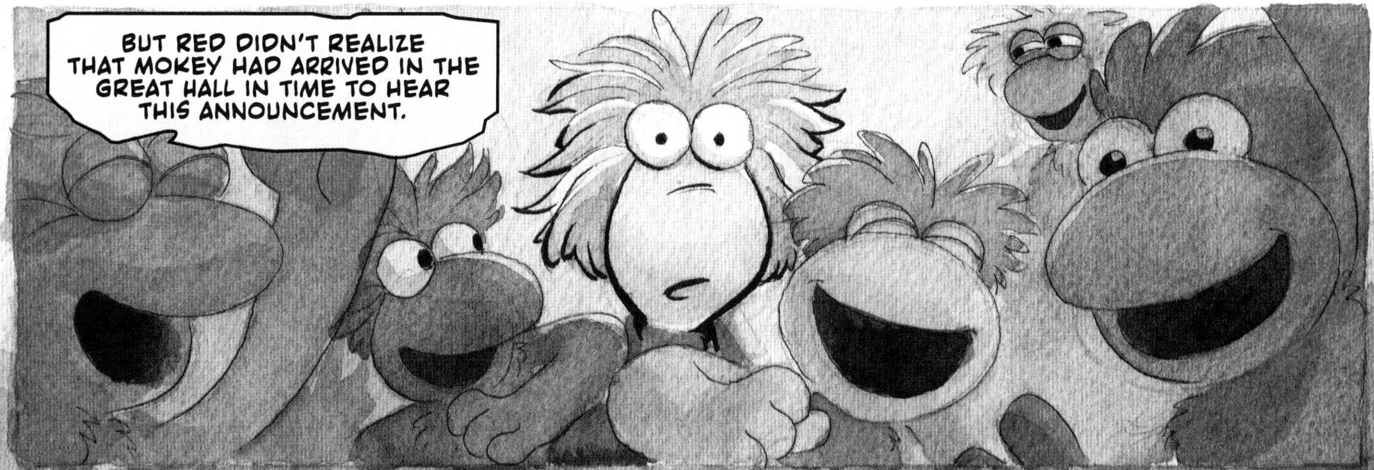
BUT RED DIDN'T REALIZE THAT MOKEY HAD ARRIVED IN THE GREAT HALL IN TIME TO HEAR THIS ANNOUNCEMENT.

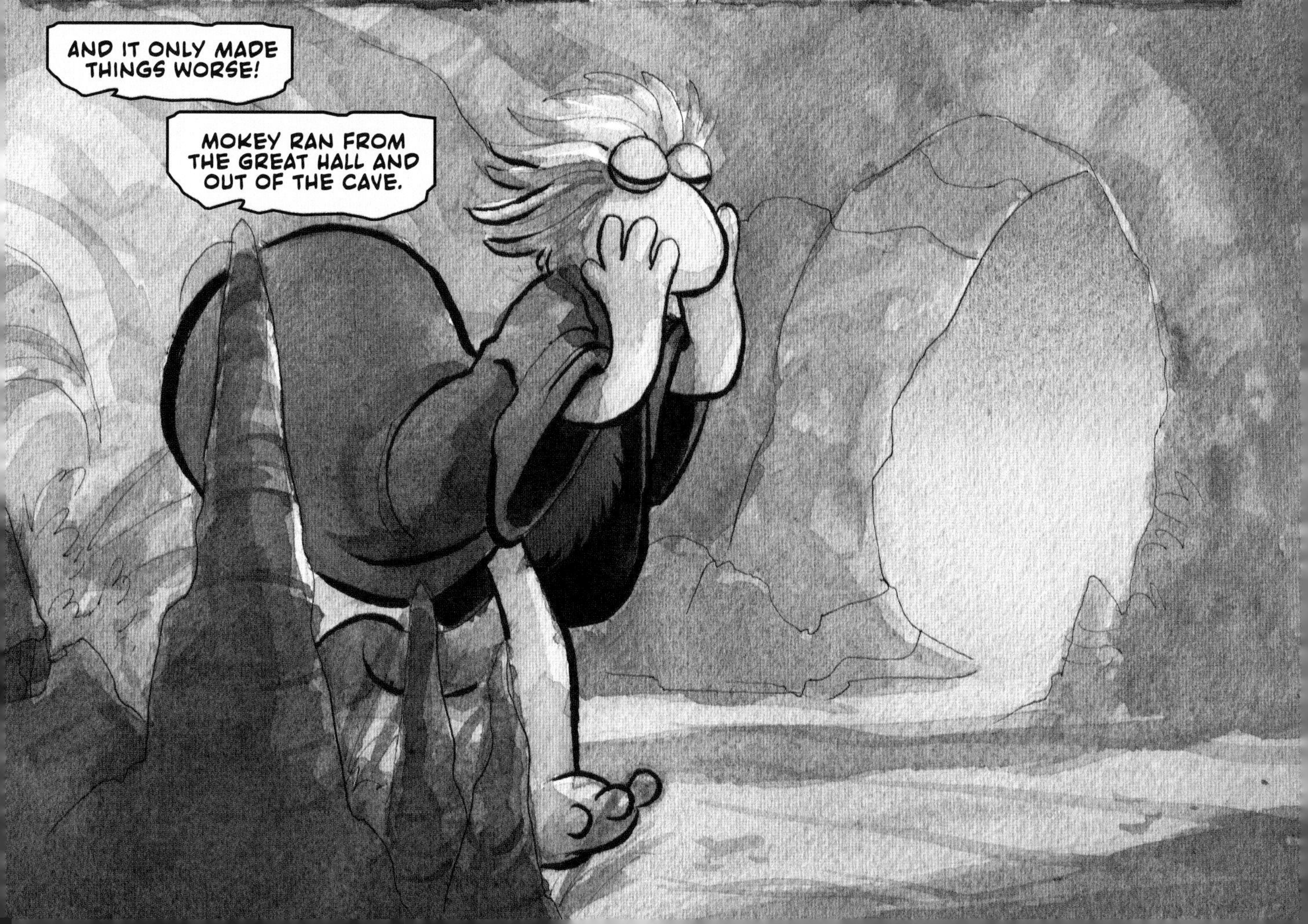
AND IT ONLY MADE THINGS WORSE!
MOKEY RAN FROM THE GREAT HALL AND OUT OF THE CAVE.

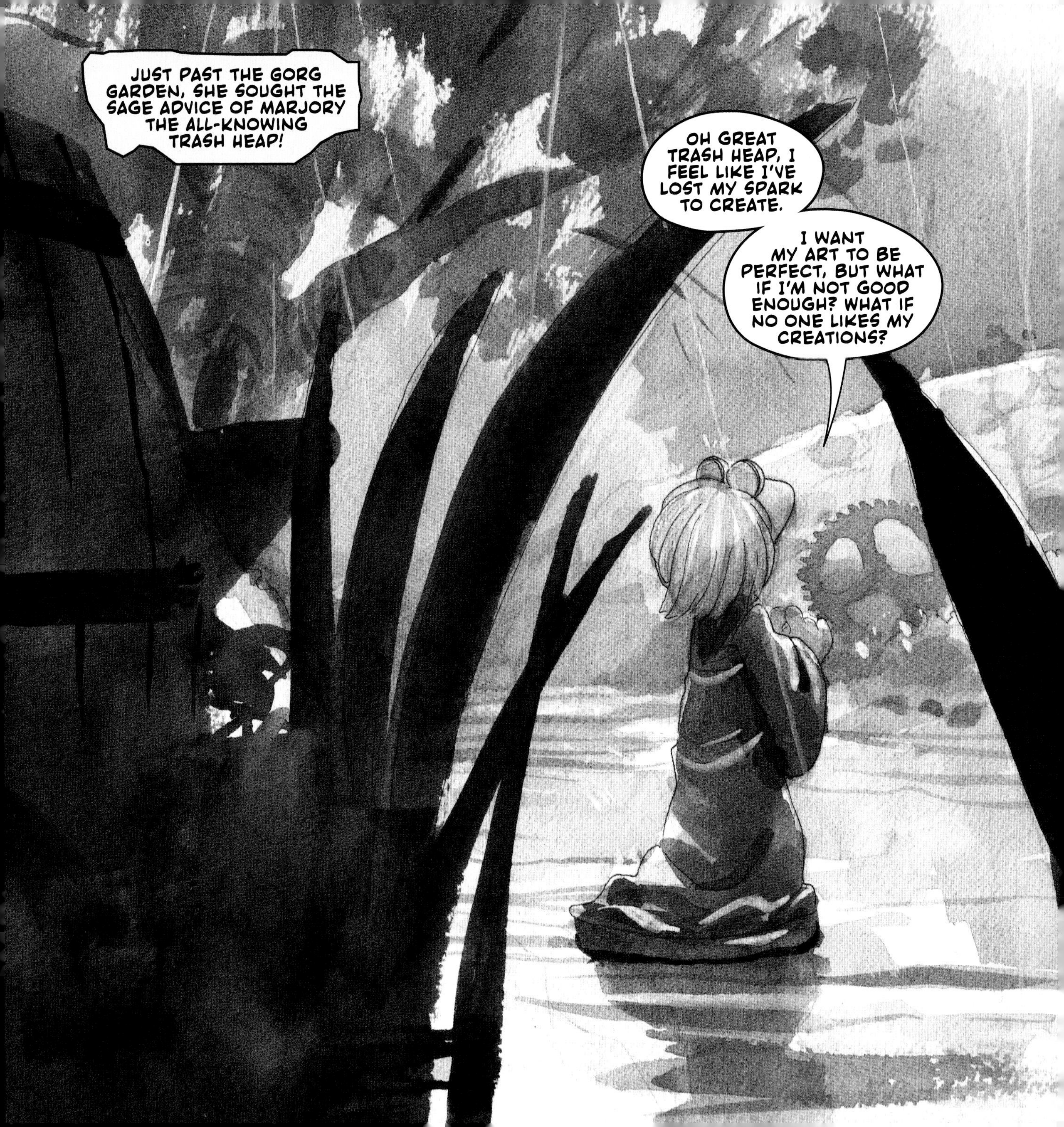
JUST PAST THE GORG GARDEN, SHE SOUGHT THE SAGE ADVICE OF MARJORY THE ALL-KNOWING TRASH HEAP!
OH GREAT TRASH HEAP, I FEEL LIKE I'VE LOST MY SPARK TO CREATE.
I WANT MY ART TO BE PERFECT, BUT WHAT IF I'M NOT GOOD ENOUGH? WHAT IF NO ONE LIKES MY CREATIONS?

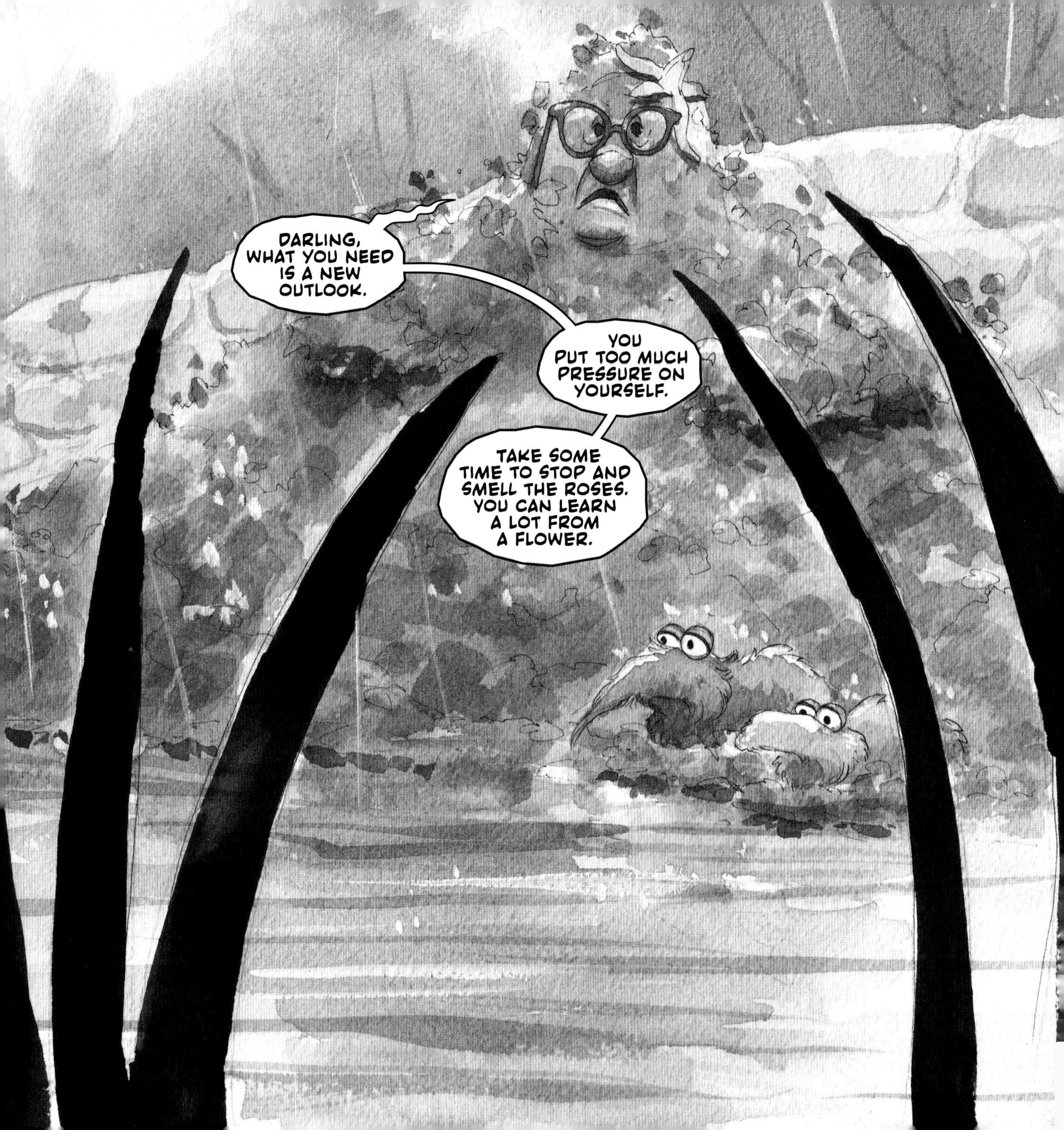
DARLING, WHAT YOU NEED IS A NEW OUTLOOK.
YOU PUT TOO MUCH PRESSURE ON YOURSELF.
TAKE SOME TIME TO STOP AND SMELL THE ROSES. YOU CAN LEARN A LOT FROM A FLOWER.

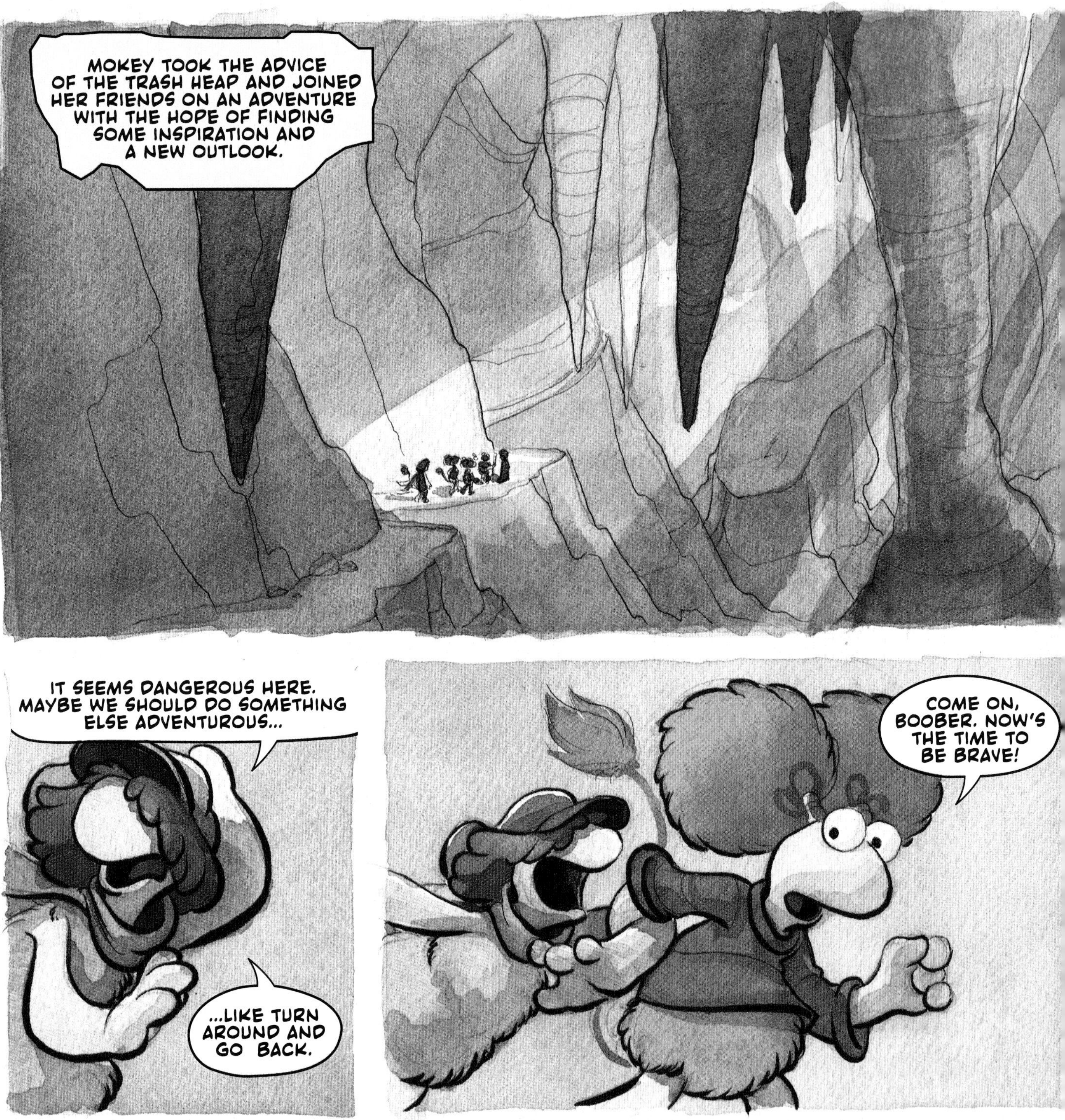
MOKEY TOOK THE ADVICE OF THE TRASH HEAP AND JOINED HER FRIENDS ON AN ADVENTURE WITH THE HOPE OF FINDING SOME INSPIRATION AND A NEW OUTLOOK.
IT SEEMS DANGEROUS HERE. MAYBE WE SHOULD DO SOMETHING ELSE ADVENTUROUS...
...LIKE TURN AROUND AND GO BACK.
COME ON, BOOBER. NOW'S THE TIME TO BE BRAVE!

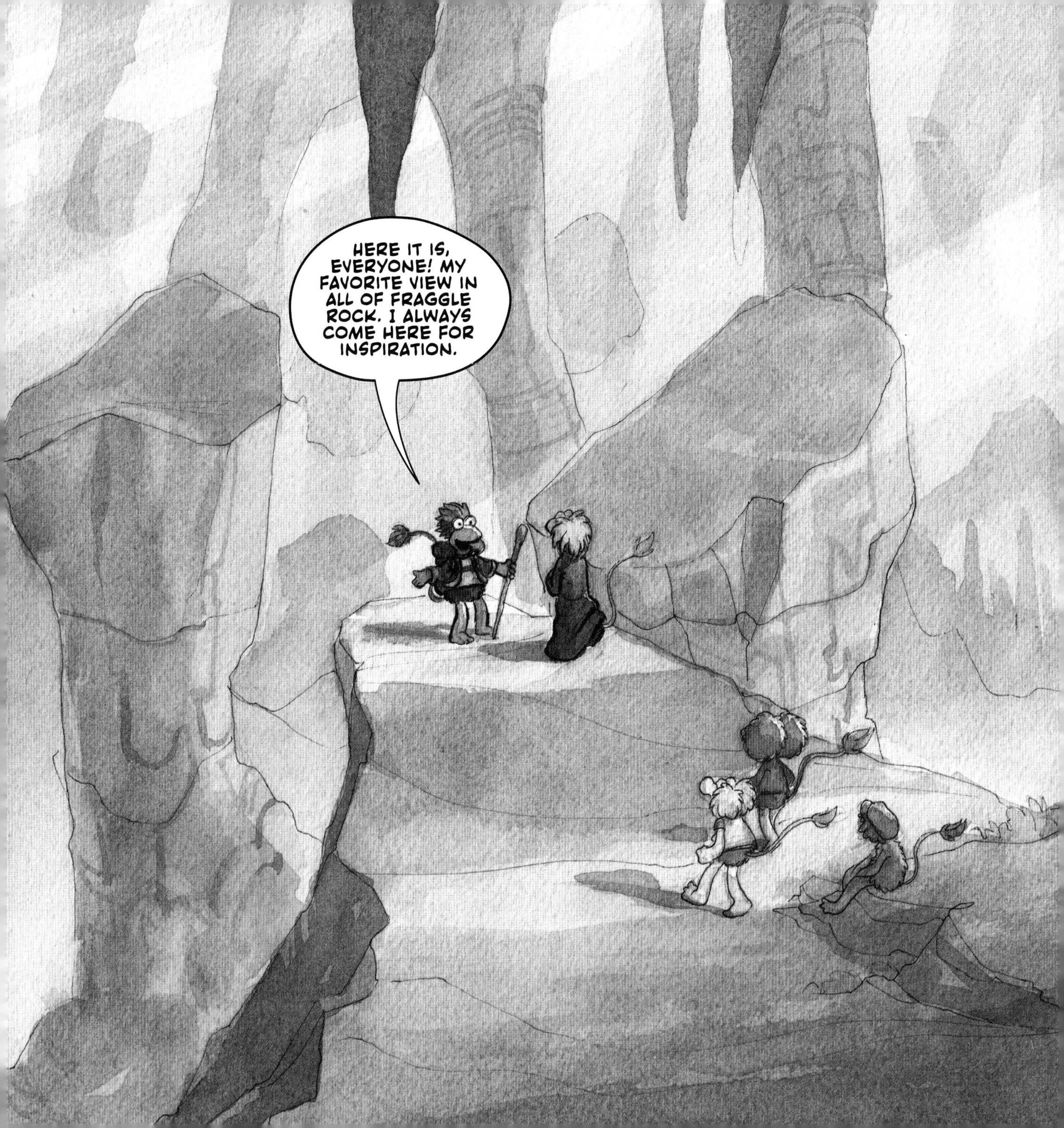
HERE IT IS, EVERYONE! MY FAVORITE VIEW IN ALL OF FRAGGLE ROCK. I ALWAYS COME HERE FOR INSPIRATION.

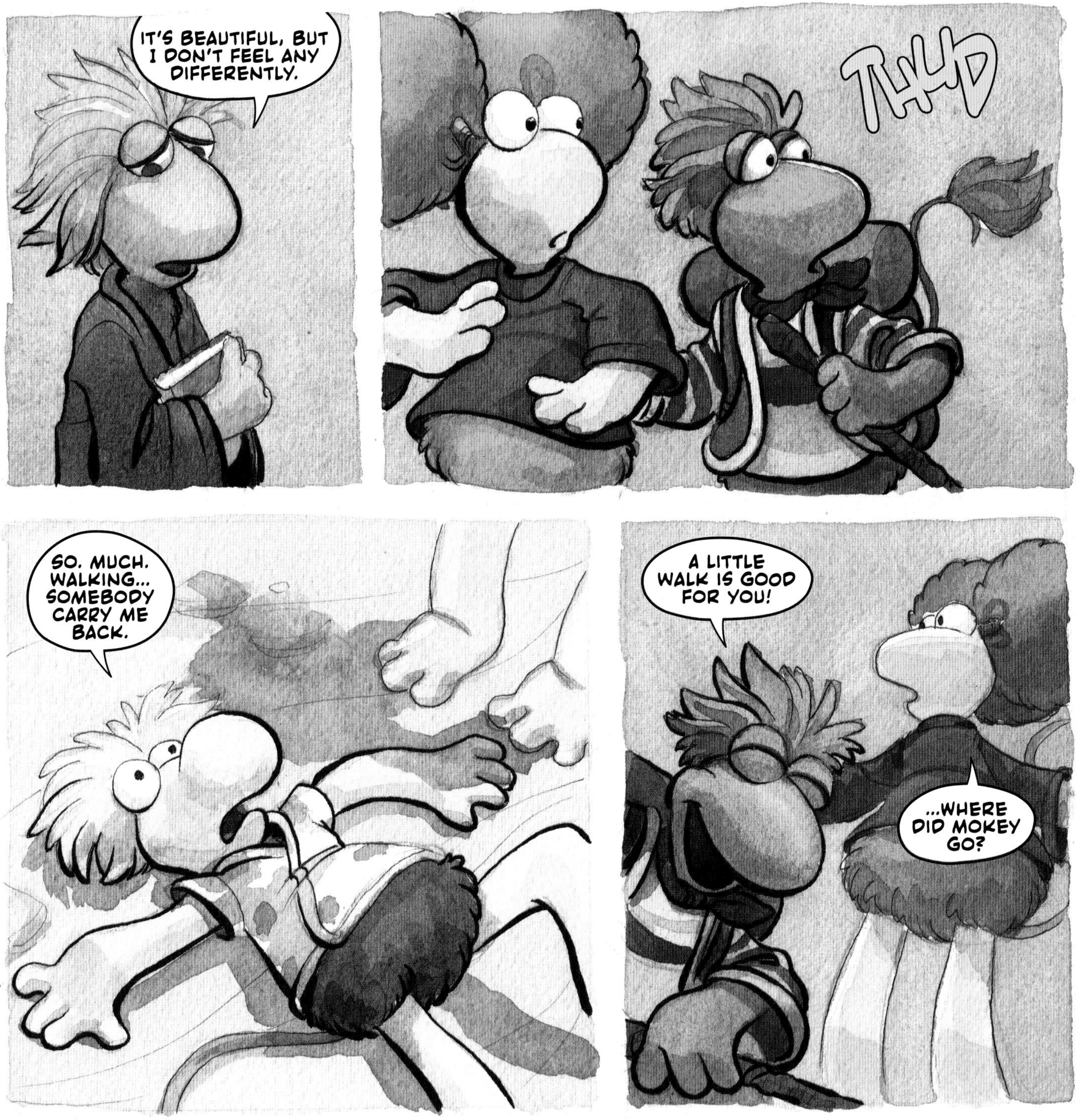
IT'S BEAUTIFUL, BUT I DON'T FEEL ANY DIFFERENTLY.
THUD
SO. MUCH. WALKING... SOMEBODY CARRY ME BACK.
A LITTLE WALK IS GOOD FOR YOU!
...WHERE DID MOKEY GO?

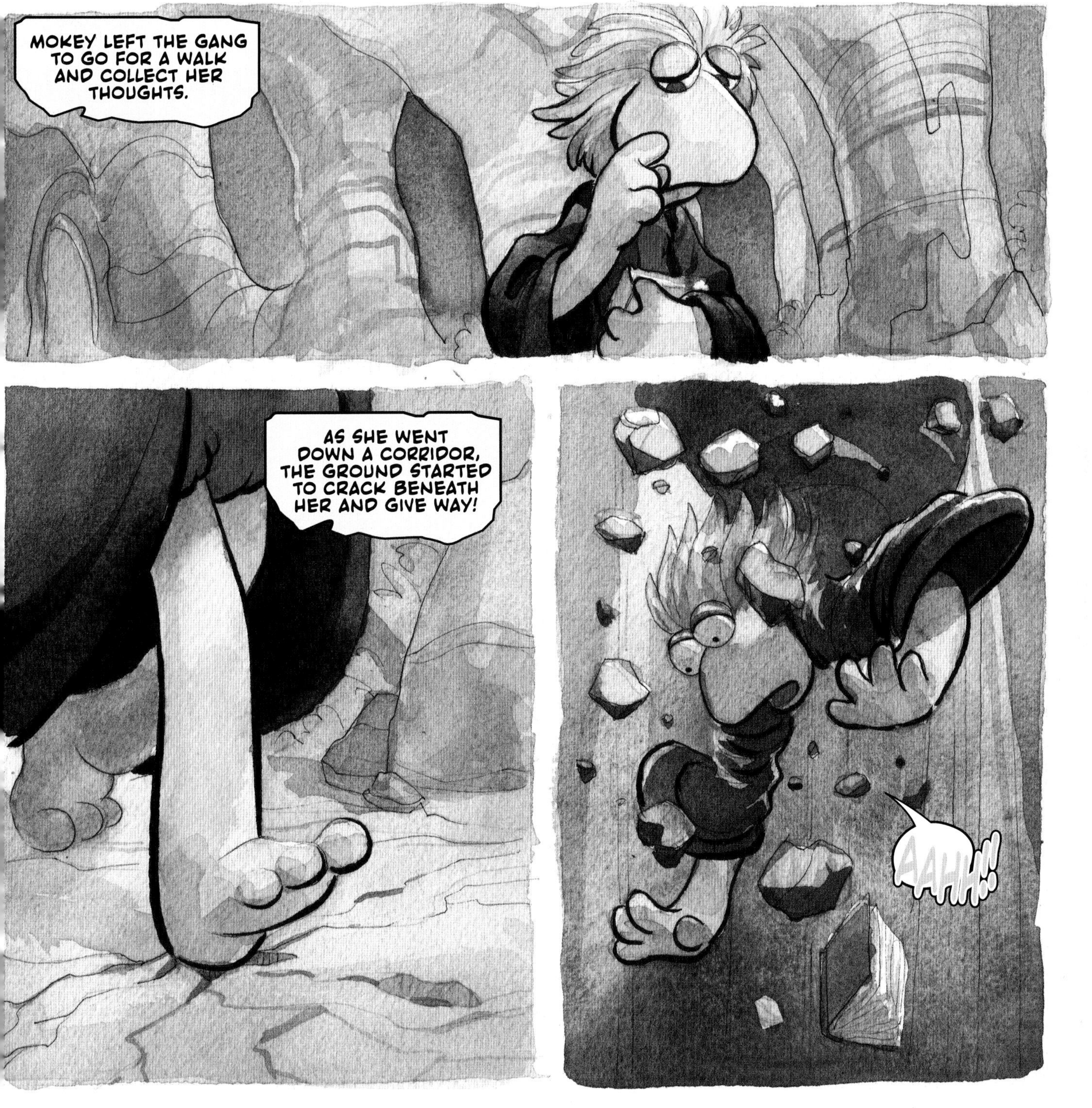
MOKEY LEFT THE GANG TO GO FOR A WALK AND COLLECT HER THOUGHTS.
AS SHE WENT DOWN A CORRIDOR, THE GROUND STARTED TO CRACK BENEATH HER AND GIVE WAY!
AAHH!!

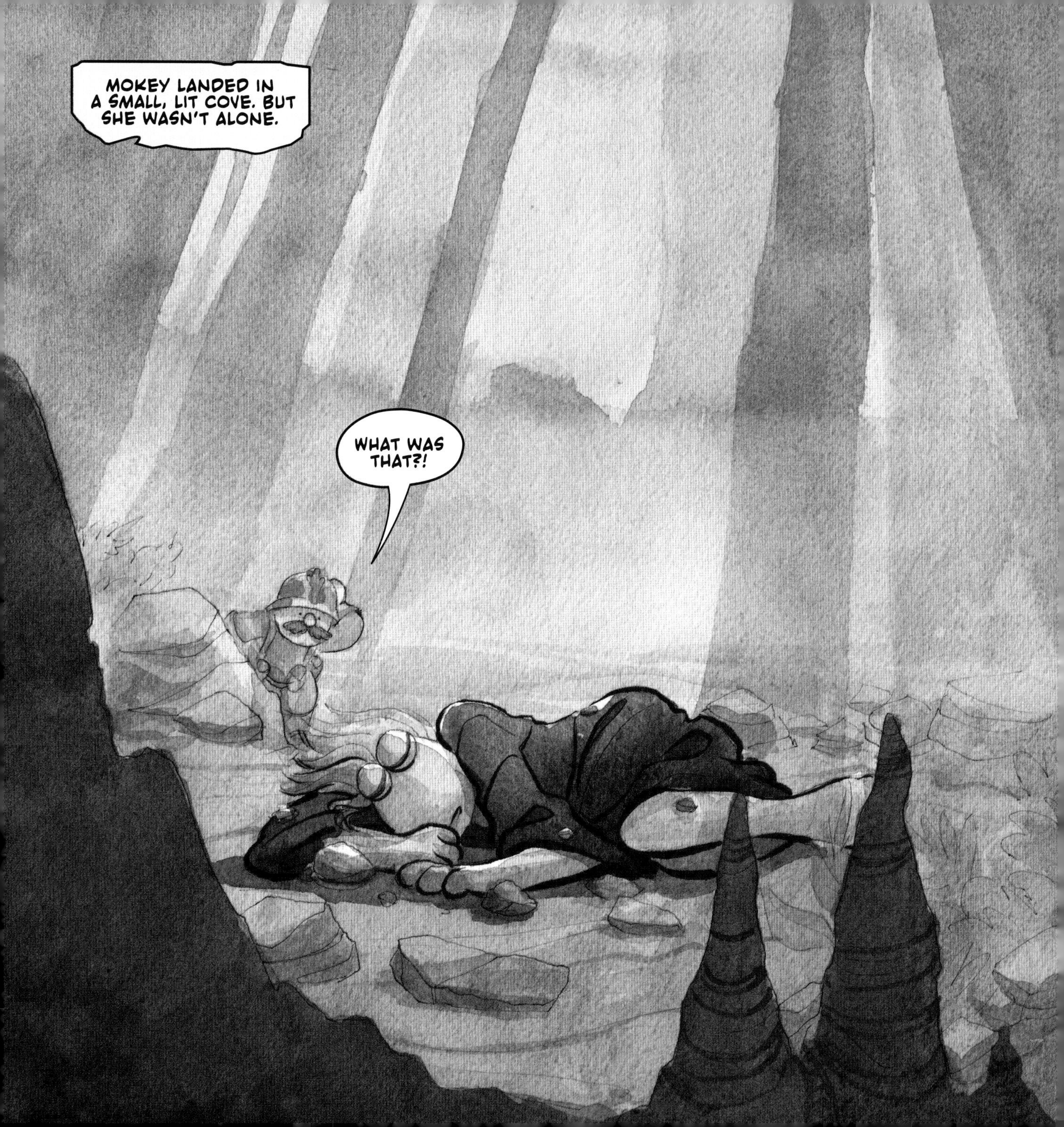
MOKEY LANDED IN A SMALL, LIT COVE. BUT SHE WASN'T ALONE.
WHAT WAS THAT?!

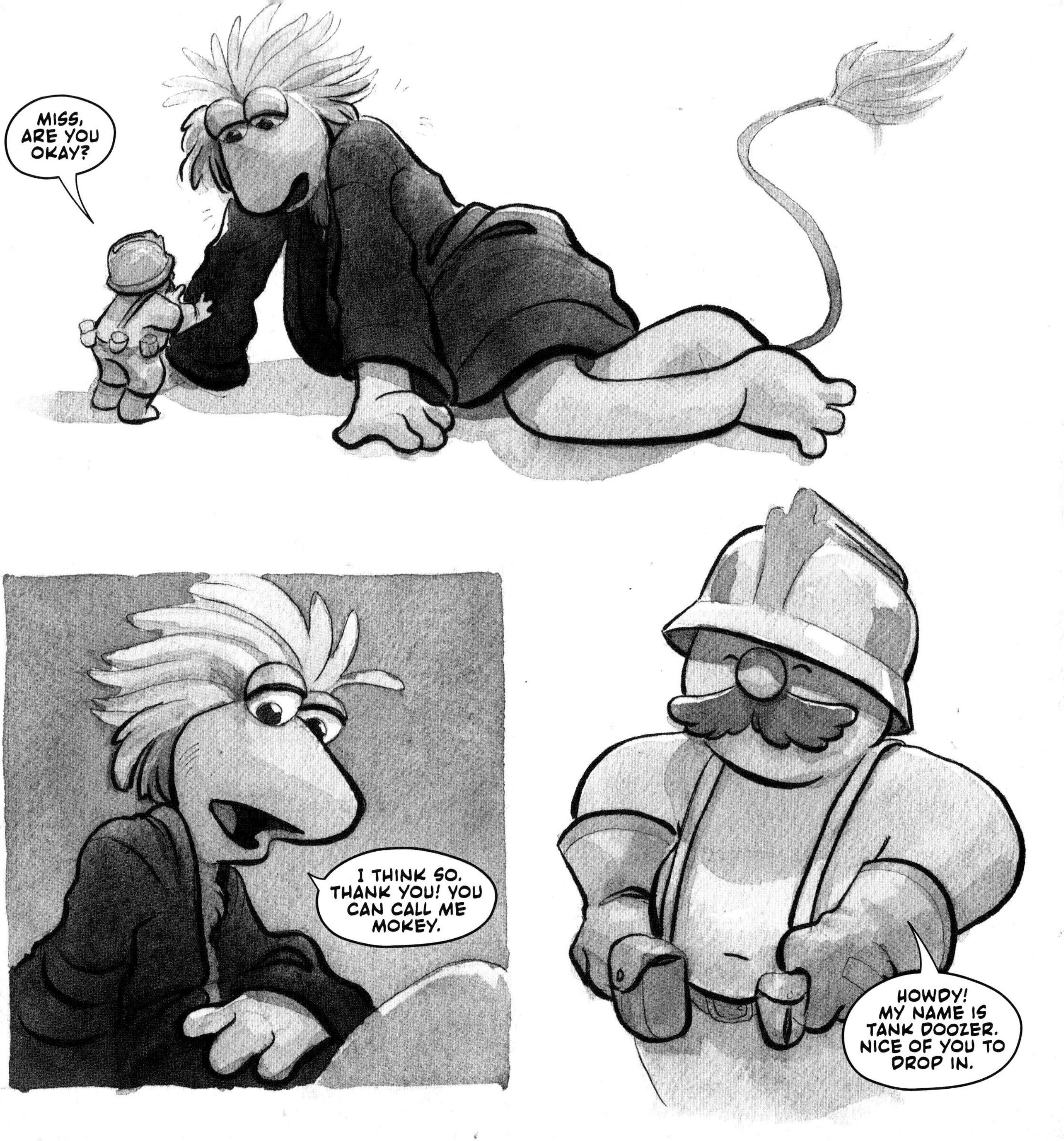
MISS, ARE YOU OKAY?
I THINK SO. THANK YOU! YOU CAN CALL ME MOKEY.
HOWDY! MY NAME IS TANK DOOZER. NICE OF YOU TO DROP IN.

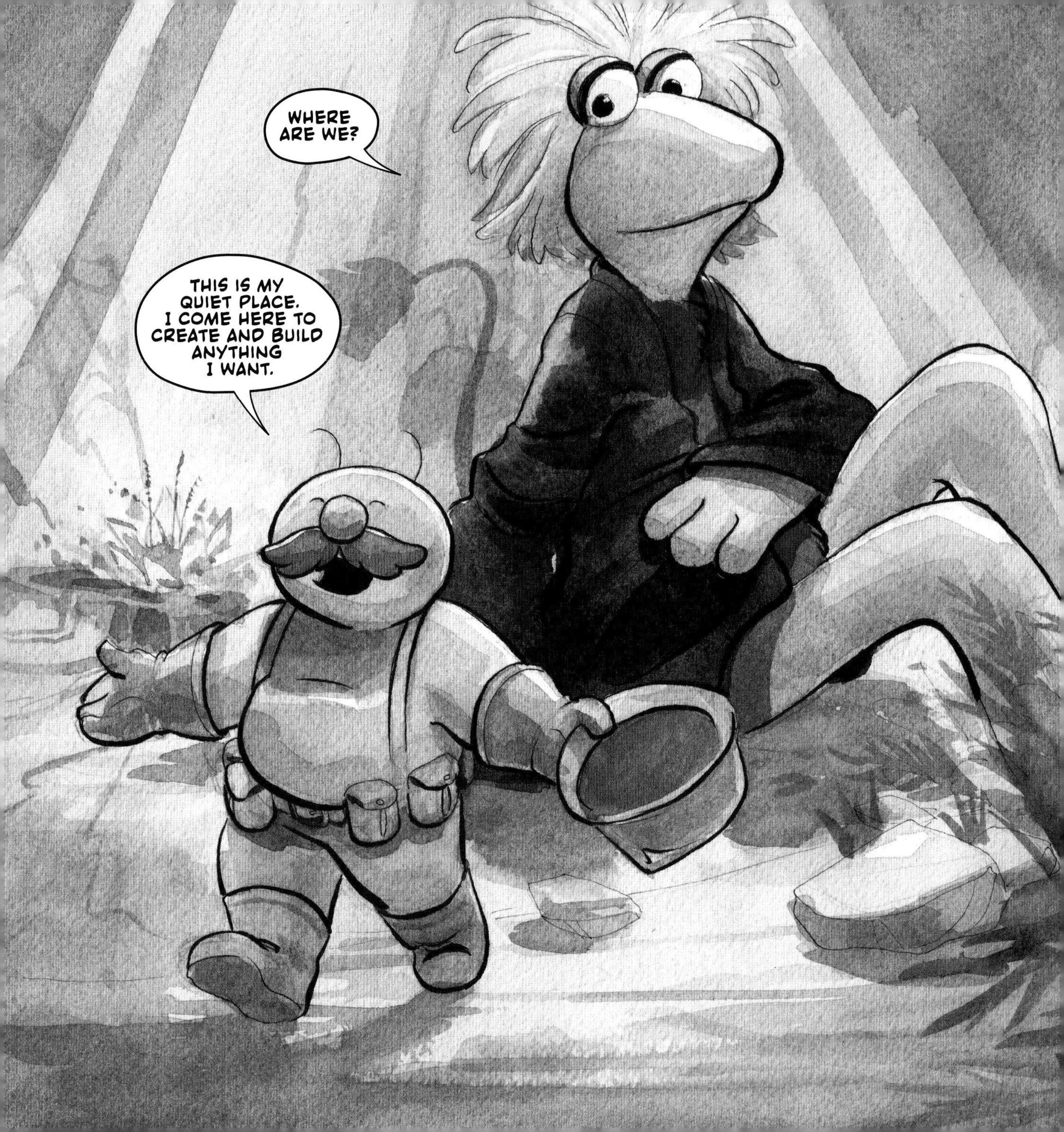
WHERE ARE WE?
THIS IS MY QUIET PLACE. I COME HERE TO CREATE AND BUILD ANYTHING I WANT.

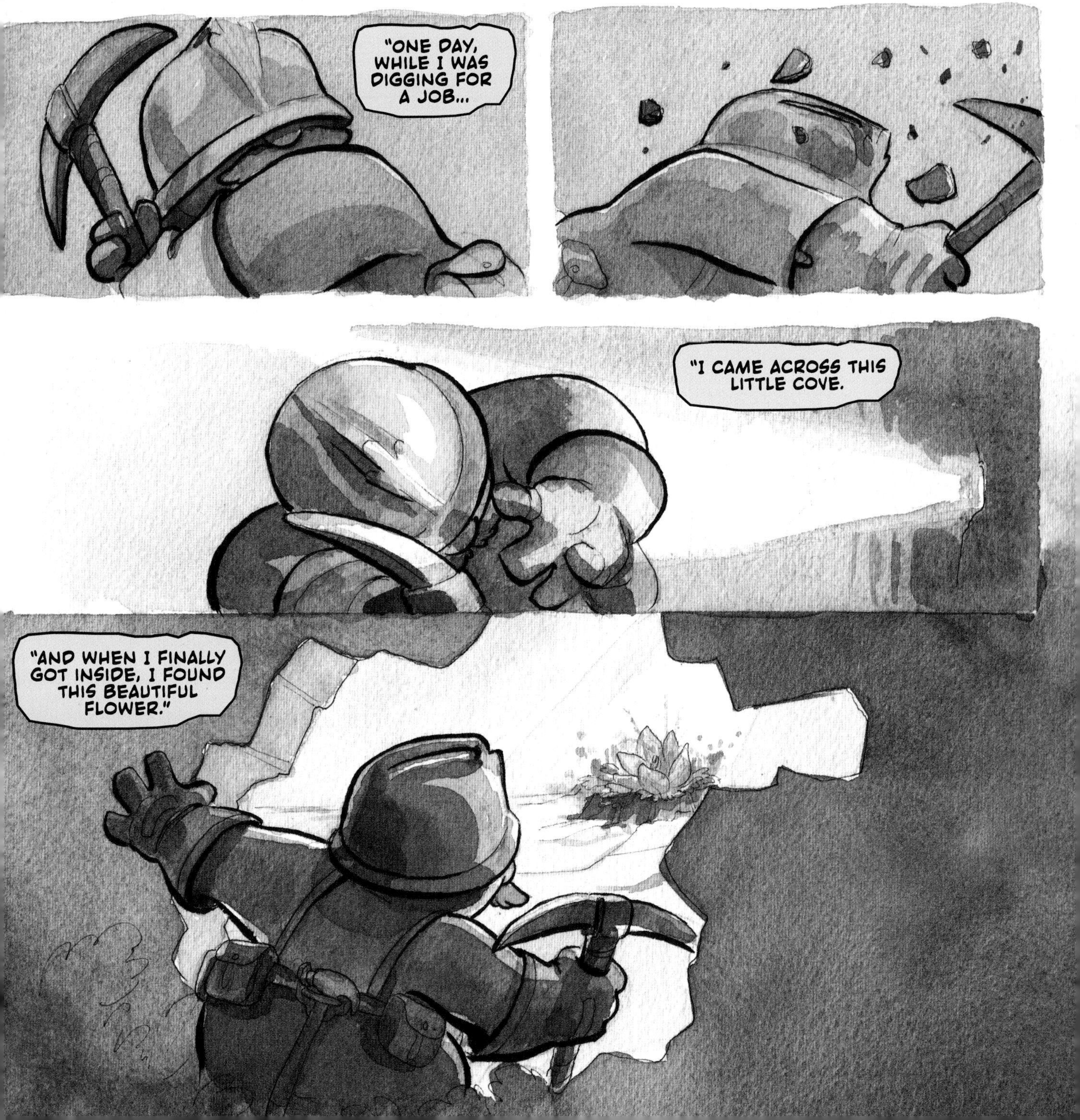
"ONE DAY, WHILE I WAS DIGGING FOR A JOB...
"I CAME ACROSS THIS LITTLE COVE.
"AND WHEN I FINALLY GOT INSIDE, I FOUND THIS BEAUTIFUL FLOWER."

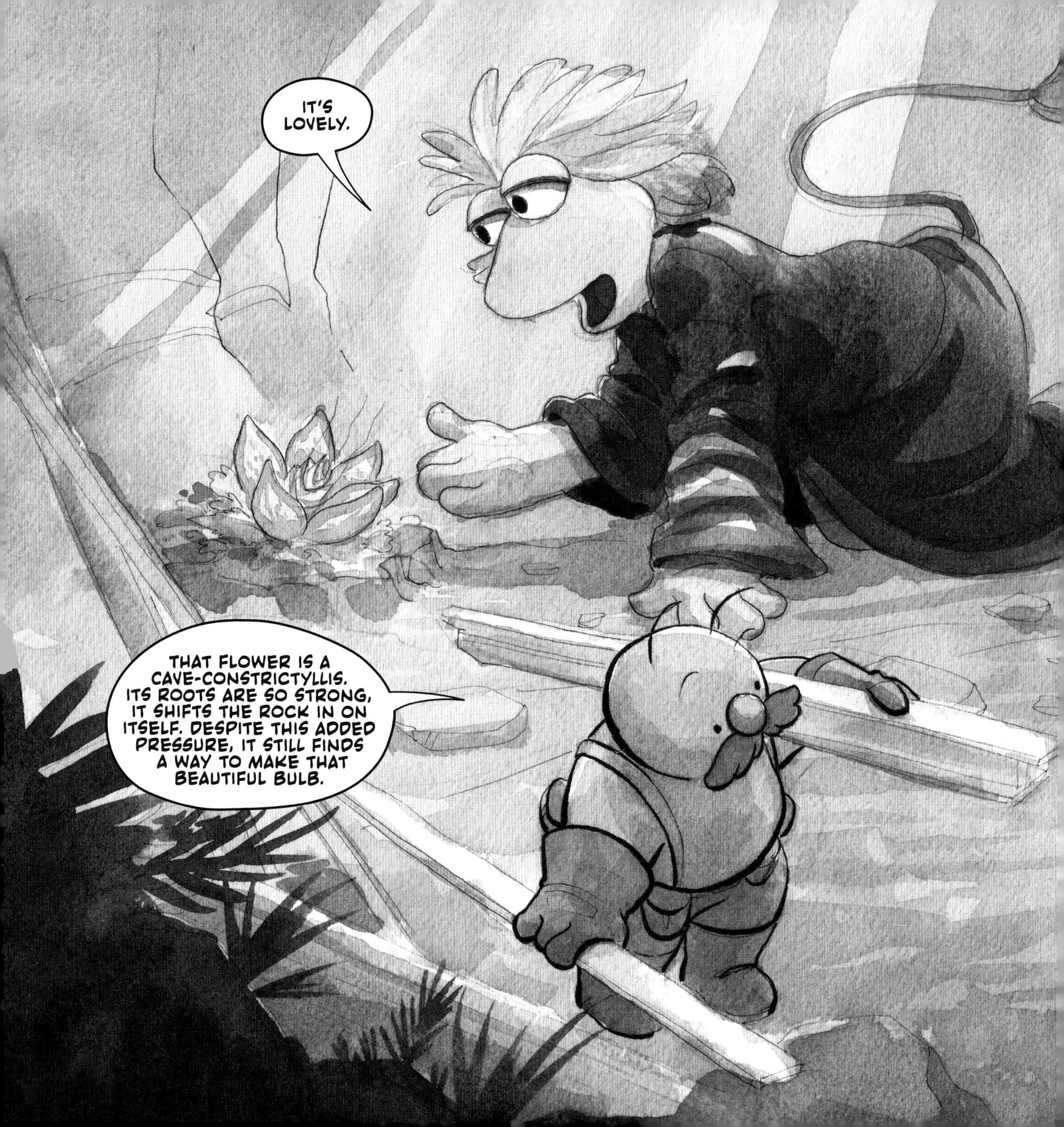
IT'S LOVELY.
THAT FLOWER IS A CAVE-CONSTRICTYLLIS. ITS ROOTS ARE SO STRONG, IT SHIFTS THE ROCK IN ON ITSELF. DESPITE THIS ADDED PRESSURE, IT STILL FINDS A WAY TO MAKE THAT BEAUTIFUL BULB.

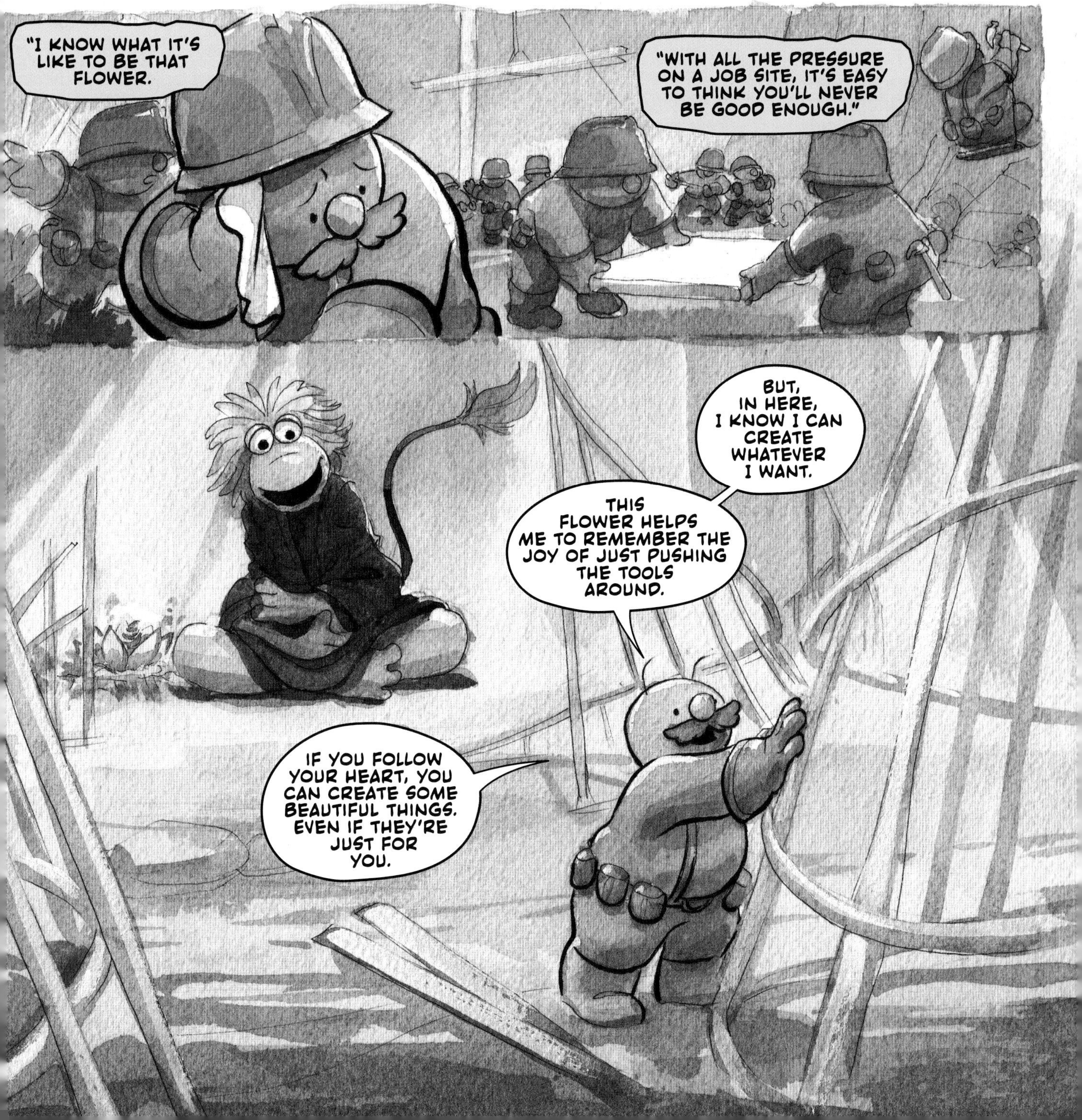
"I KNOW WHAT IT'S LIKE TO BE THAT FLOWER.
"WITH ALL THE PRESSURE ON A JOB SITE, IT'S EASY TO THINK YOU'LL NEVER BE GOOD ENOUGH."
BUT, IN HERE, I KNOW I CAN CREATE WHATEVER I WANT.
THIS FLOWER HELPS ME TO REMEMBER THE JOY OF JUST PUSHING THE TOOLS AROUND.
IF YOU FOLLOW YOUR HEART, YOU CAN CREATE SOME BEAUTIFUL THINGS. EVEN IF THEY'RE JUST FOR YOU.

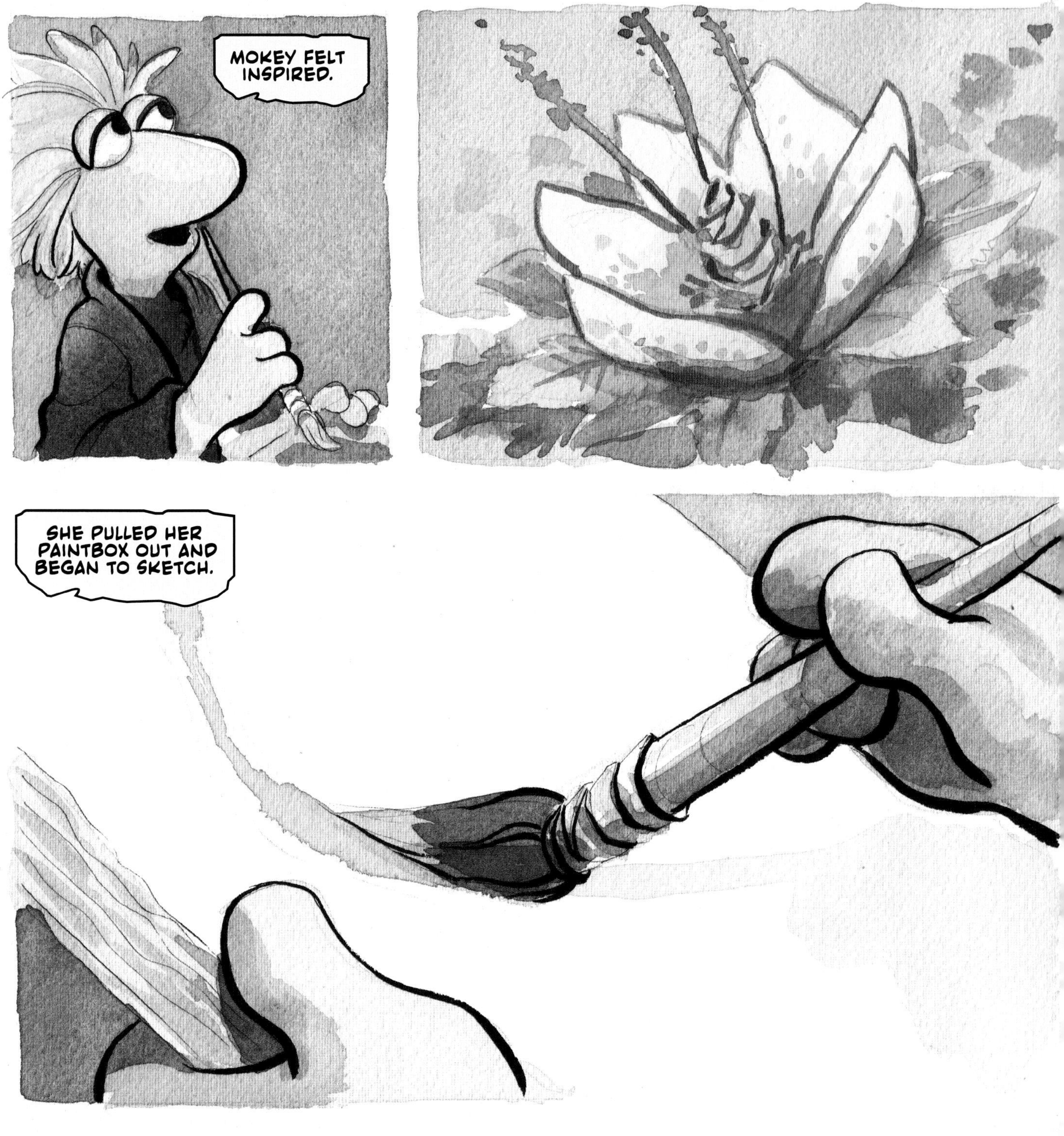
MOKEY FELT INSPIRED.
SHE PULLED HER PAINTBOX OUT AND BEGAN TO SKETCH.

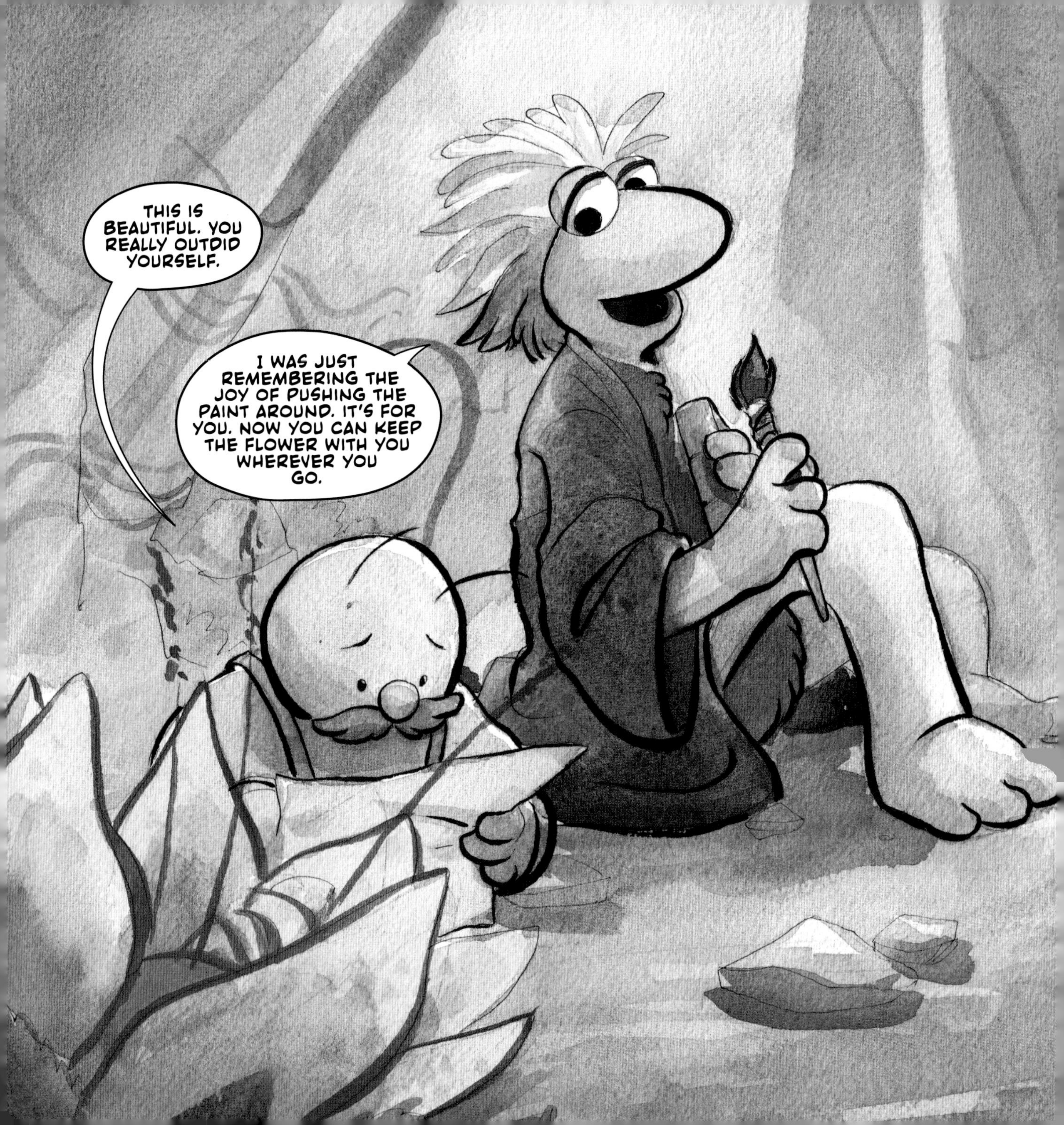
THIS IS BEAUTIFUL. YOU REALLY OUTDID YOURSELF.
I WAS JUST REMEMBERING THE JOY OF PUSHING THE PAINT AROUND. IT'S FOR YOU. NOW YOU CAN KEEP THE FLOWER WITH YOU WHEREVER YOU GO.

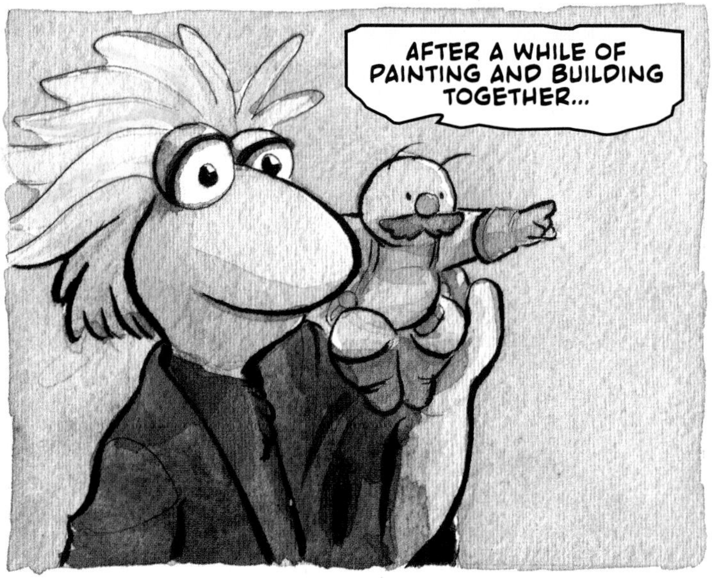
AFTER A WHILE OF PAINTING AND BUILDING TOGETHER...

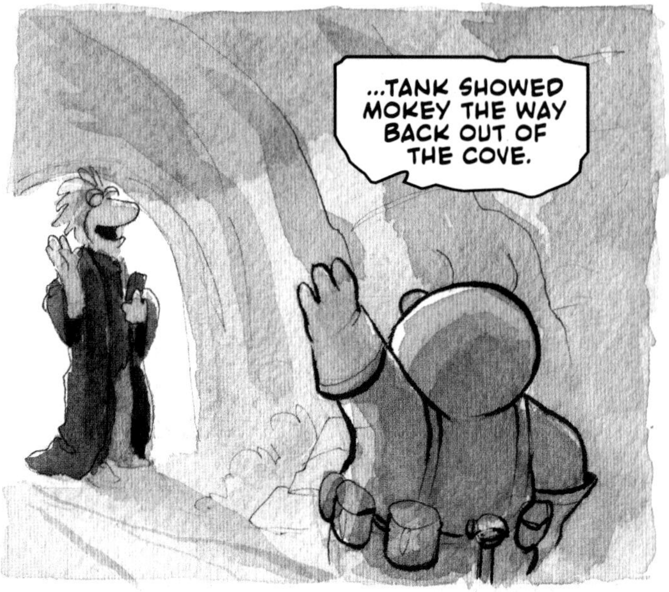
...TANK SHOWED MOKEY THE WAY BACK OUT OF THE COVE.

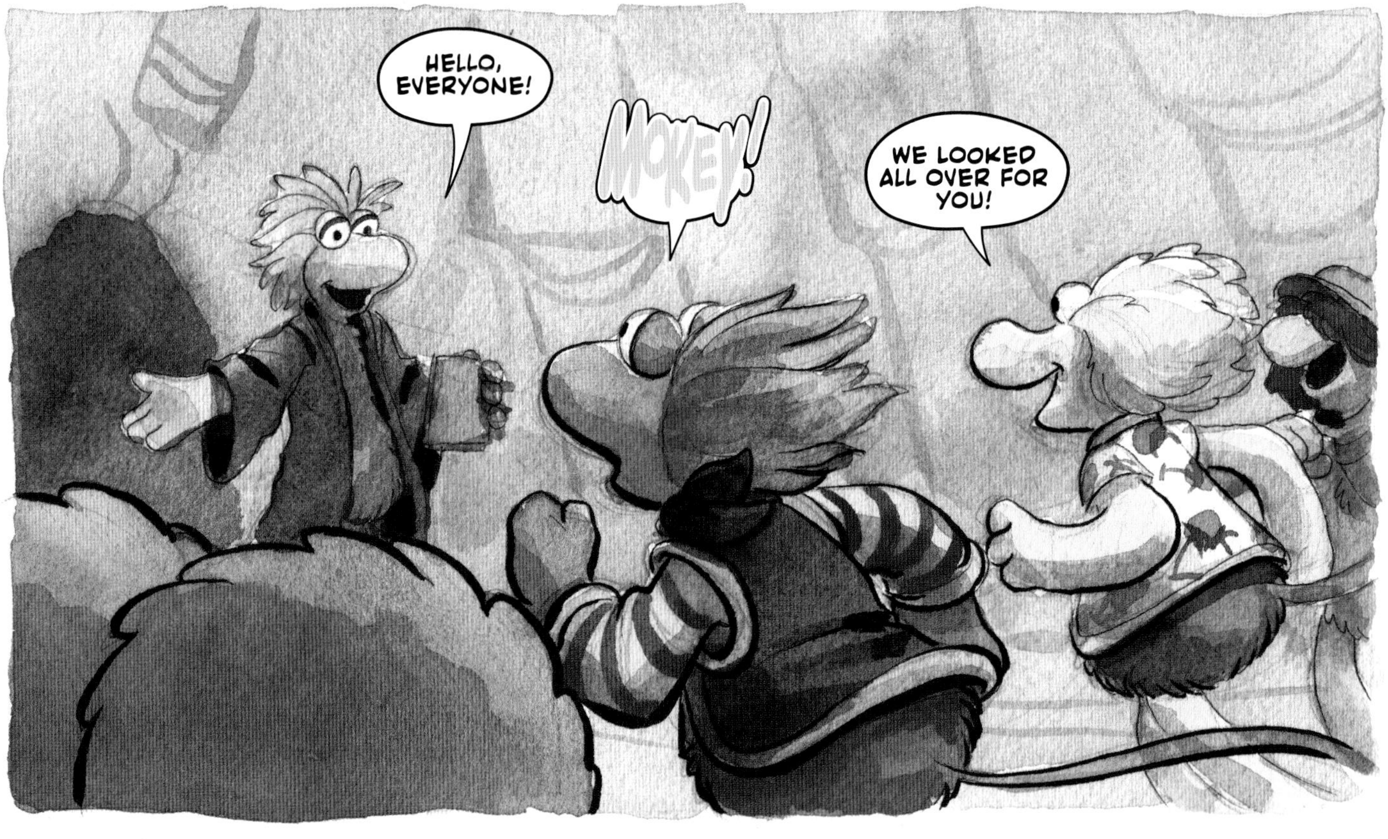
HELLO, EVERYONE!
MOKEY!
WE LOOKED ALL OVER FOR YOU!

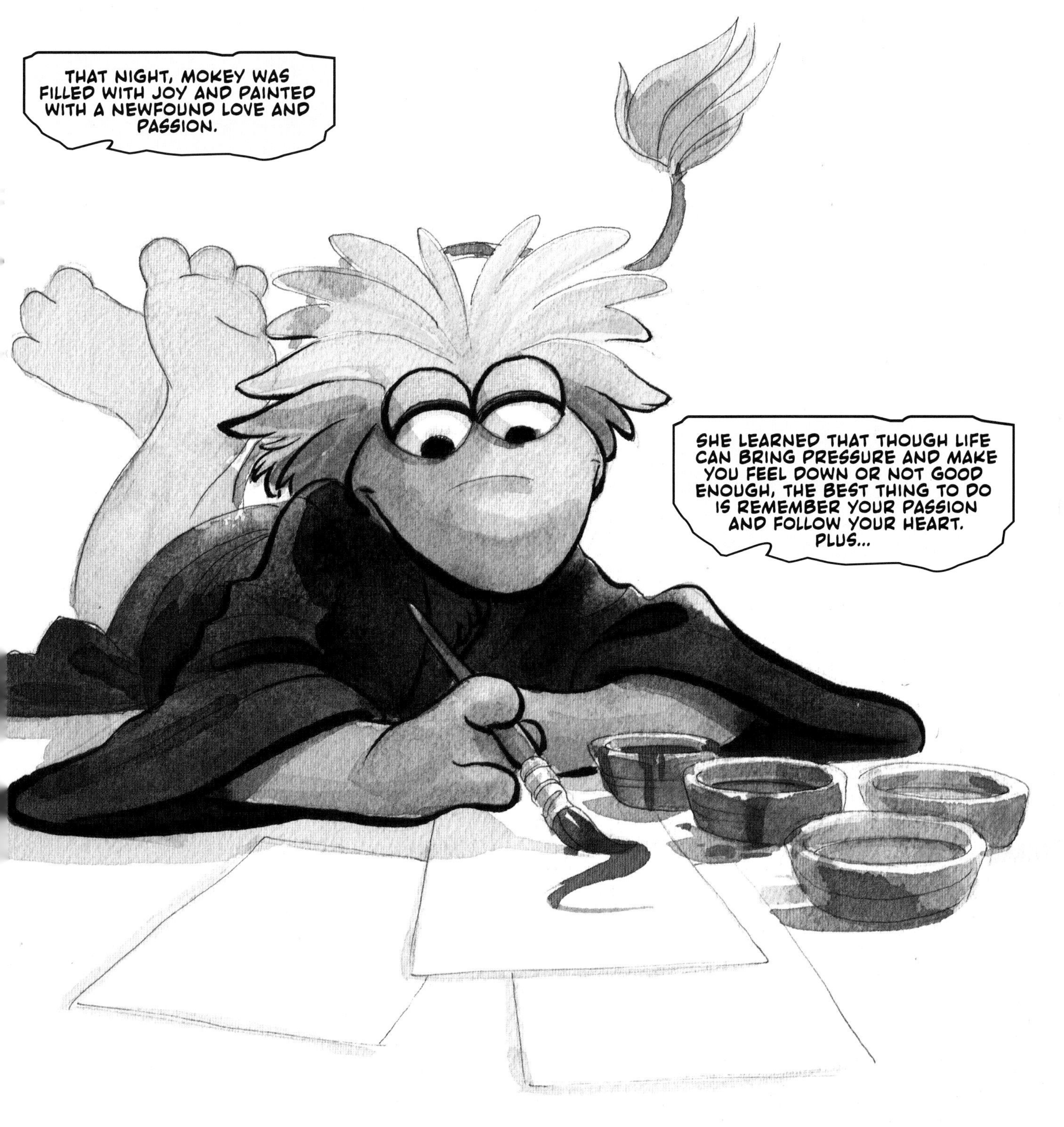
THAT NIGHT, MOKEY WAS FILLED WITH JOY AND PAINTED WITH A NEWFOUND LOVE AND PASSION.
SHE LEARNED THAT THOUGH LIFE CAN BRING PRESSURE AND MAKE YOU FEEL DOWN OR NOT GOOD ENOUGH, THE BEST THING TO DO IS REMEMBER YOUR PASSION AND FOLLOW YOUR HEART. PLUS...

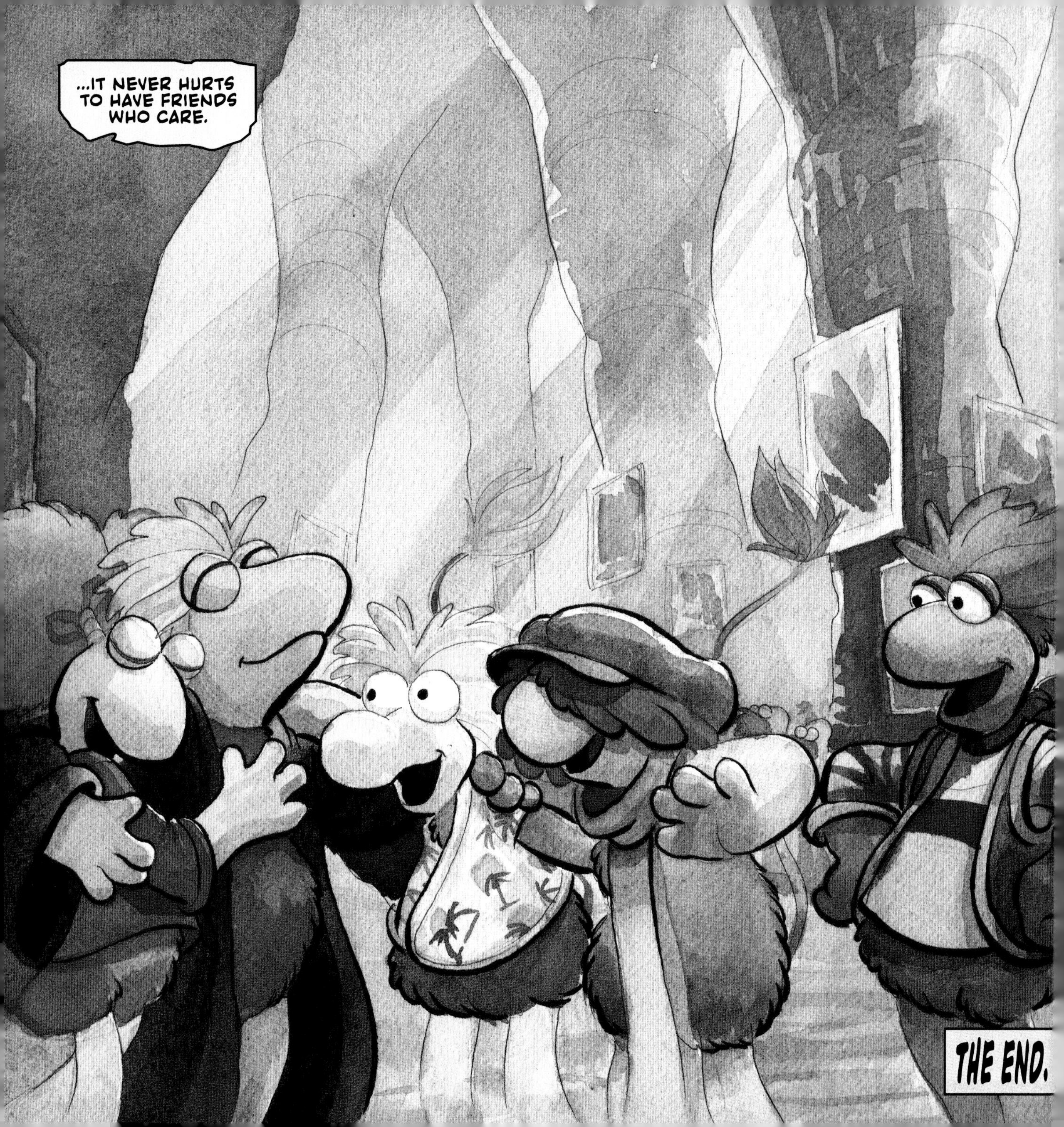
...IT NEVER HURTS TO HAVE FRIENDS WHO CARE.
THE END.

DISCOVER

THE WORLD OF JIM HENSON

Jim Henson's
TALE OF SAND
The lost screenplay by JIM HENSON and JERRY JUHL
As realized by RAMÓN K. PÉREZ

Jim Henson's
LABYRINTH
ARTIST TRIBUTE

Jim Henson's
THE POWER OF THE
DARK CRYSTAL
Simon Spurrier
Kelly Matthews
Nichole Matthews

Jim Henson's
THE STORYTELLER
Dragons

Jim Henson's
The Dark Crystal
TALES

Jim Henson's
LABYRINTH
ADULT COLORING BOOK

ARCHAIA™

AVAILABLE AT YOUR LOCAL COMICS SHOP AND BOOKSTORE

WWW.**BOOM-STUDIOS**.COM

Jim Henson's Tale of Sand
Jim Henson, Jerry Juhl, Ramón K. Pérez
ISBN: 978-1-93639-309-1 | $29.95 US

Jim Henson's The Dark Crystal: Creation Myths
Brian Froud, Alex Sheikman, Joshua Dysart, and others
Volume 1
ISBN: 978-1-60886-704-2 | $14.99 US
Volume 2
ISBN: 978-1-60886-887-2 | $14.99 US
Volume 3
ISBN: 978-1-60886-906-0 | $14.99 US

Jim Henson's The Power of the Dark Crystal
Simon Spurrier, Kelly and Nichole Matthews
Volume 1
ISBN: 978-1-60886-992-3 | $24.99 US

Jim Henson's The Dark Crystal Tales
Cory Godbey
ISBN: 978-1-60886-845-2 | $16.99 US

Jim Henson's Labyrinth Artist Tribute
Michael Allred, Dave McKean, Faith Erin Hicks, and others
ISBN: 978-1-60886-897-1 | $24.99 US

Jim Henson's Labyrinth Adult Coloring Book
Jorge Corona, Jay Fosgitt, Phil Murphy
ISBN: 978-1-68415-111-0 | $16.99 US

Jim's Henson's The Musical Monsters of Turkey Hollow
Jim Henson, Jerry Juhl, Roger Langridge
ISBN: 978-1-60886-434-8 | $24.99 US

Jim Henson's The Storyteller: Witches
S.M. Vidaurri, Kyla Vanderklugt, Matthew Dow Smith, Jeff Stokely
ISBN: 978-1-60886-747-9 | $24.99 US

Jim Henson's The Storyteller: Dragons
Daniel Bayliss, Jorge Corona, Hannah Christensen, Nathan Pride
ISBN: 978-1-60886-874-2 | $24.99 US

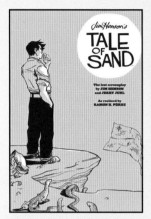

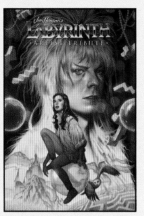

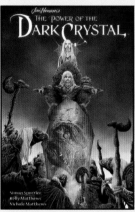

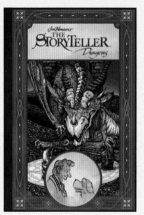

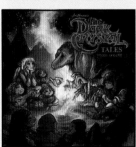

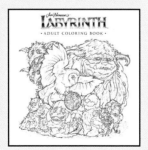

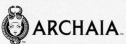